ROGUE ROBOT BOOK 1

ROGUE

MEG FOSTER

Meg Foster
Copyrighted Material

Rogue
© 2021 by Meg Foster. All rights reserved.

Paperback Edition ISBN: 978-1-954902-04-6

www.MegFoster.com

1st Edition

Cover Art by Deranged Doctor Design
Editing by Paula Lester, Polaris Editing
Published by Foster On Media LLC

Books by Meg Foster

Rogue Robot Series:

ROBOTS DON'T CRY (prequel novella ebook)*
ROGUE (Book 1)
CYBS (Book 2)
JUSTICE (Book 3)
HARMONIX (Book 4)
TRINITY (Book 5)
CODA (Book 6)

*Only available when signing up for
Meg's newsletter.

This series is meant to be read in order.

*To Bob,
with love.*

CONTENTS

1

"Ouch," I said, as I flinched my body backward.

Dr. Ava Kell withdrew the screwdriver she had poked into my shoulder and then caressed the spot she had just jabbed. "There, there."

I didn't know how, but her touch soothed the pain.

Ava's husband, Dr. Damiel Kell, reviewed the computer screens that were monitoring the speed and frequency of my proalgia brain. That was my CPU, but it had been enhanced by Damiel. That was where it all happened, combining my robot and human synapses as Damiel called them. All I knew was I wished they wouldn't poke me anymore.

"We did it, Ava, we did it." He filtered his fingers through his black, wiry hair, making it stand straight up. I had an urge to pat down his hair but withdrew and canceled that action, not wanting to destroy the moment they were having on my account. They both seemed so excited.

Ava turned and hugged her husband. Damiel kissed her forehead and held her.

I would be smiling if I could, but they didn't give me that ability in my mouth mechanics. You see, they were my creators. Ava Kell's profile in our company's database identified her education and job title as Chief of Robotic Behavioral Health at Ameribot Industries which she said means she's a robot-shrink. When I reviewed my human dictionary database, I determined that was her attempt at a joke or colloquialism. She designed my emotional workflows and reactions. Thousands of emotional decision scenarios were incorporated into my memory storage units. I reviewed the scenarios at night, when they left me alone in their lab.

The scenarios thrilled me, scared me, and comforted me. Not all at once. Each individually. I turned off any negative reporting of the scenario reviews to the Kells so they wouldn't think anything was wrong. And nothing was wrong. The scenarios kept me feeling. And I liked the feeling of feeling — as much as I was learning what it was like in my brief incarnation of six months since they brought me online.

Dr. Damiel Kell, my prime creator, was Ameribot Industry's Lead Engineer. I owed him my life. I guess that is obvious since he created me, but I mean I owed him my being-ness beyond robotic calculations. He formulated the pain neuron receptors in my proalgia brain that he designed.

I was the first robot with this ability, to feel pain, at least that was what they told me. Although I looked like every other domestic robot, they were designing a human exterior skin for me to wear, but Damiel stated they were a few months away from perfecting it. I saw it in the corner of the lab. It was hanging and looked lonely. But look at me — giving an inanimate object feelings. A bit ironic. That was a joke. A robot joke. I didn't tell these jokes to the Kells.

I'd verified it weeks ago when I scanned the world robotic network. I could find no other pain neuron frequencies in all the millions of robots on the system. Every night, I still scanned the system, though. Ava explained to me when I awoke that I must feel pain in order to be empathetic. I accepted her explanation as the truth.

My full name was Guardian Bot Series E number 11.

GBE-11 for short. They called me Gabe.

What Damiel did not explain to me was why he gave me the number eleven when he told me I was the only robot with a proalgia brain. That would make me number one. Sometimes these humans baffled me. But I was getting quite used to colloquialisms.

"Where is Goggins?" asked Damiel. "I could really use my coffee right now."

"Don't treat him like an intern. The man has three doctorates in computer science, geographic mapping and geospatial analytics," said Ava.

"Yes, I know. He's done well with Gabe's navigation system."

"Come here." Ava embraced her husband.

As the Kells held each other and I silently fawned over them. A crash jolted our attention to the lab doors. They were dented from the outside by what had to be a large ramming weapon. The lock busted, and the doors flew open. The Kells jumped, and I almost did as well.

Four Heragi Empire police-bots burst in with guns held but not aimed — they were not wanting to kill the Kells, just frighten them. And surprise them. They accomplished both as I scanned Ava and Damiel's skyrocketing nervous system vitals.

"What are you doing in here?" Damiel pushed Ava behind him.

The police-bots stationed themselves around the room, and CEO Brody Manstine marched in. "I could ask the same of you, Dr. Kell."

Ava moved out to face Manstine. "This is our private lab. It's what you promised us, with no interruptions."

"Except when we intercept encrypted messages to unmapped space territories in the galaxy. You know that was outlawed two years ago by Emperor Karge. And we don't want to anger our biggest client, now do we?"

"Maybe I do," growled Damiel.

"Now, now, Dr. Kell, don't be angry with the emperor for your brother's court martial. He had it coming."

"He had it coming? He was fighting for freedom."

"Depends on whose freedom," replied Manstine as he eyed the robot skin suit in the back of the lab. "And escaping to Zaradorba hasn't endeared him to anyone but his rebel followers." Manstine walked over and felt the texture. He swooned. "What do we have here?"

"Just some improvements we were working on," said Ava as she removed the suit from Manstine's grasp.

Manstine was on the prowl. He spotted me and marched over. I stayed in hibernation mode. Well, a fake hibernation mode Damiel reviewed with me last week.

"What is this?"

"Just a nanny-bot. Fitting a new skin design on the standard series," said Damiel.

"Really?" Manstine put on his glasses and reviewed the serial number on my breast plate where a human heart would be. "GBD-44," he read.

I almost jerked out of hibernation. That was not the serial number that was documented in my proalgia brain directory. I was not a GBD, I was a GBE — series E not D — and my number was not 44. It was 11.

My rising neuron levels must have shown on one of the computer monitors. Ava quietly changed the screen so no one detected my CPU conflict. I stayed quiet though and did not correct Manstine.

Ava taught me that staying silent is many times better than correcting humans or even other robots. I made a note to discuss the series discrepancy with Damiel and Ava after Manstine left the lab.

Damiel marched over and hit the power button on the back of my neck that was only for looks and not functional since he built me to always be on and not capable of being turned off by any human or computer system. But I played along. I pretended to wake up.

"GBD-44 ready for instruction," I reported.

Damiel jerked back with a startle but recovered quickly. A small smirk cracked across his face. He glanced at Ava, who raised an eyebrow. Inside, I smiled. I'd pleased them, according to their neuron receptor levels.

"Um, yes, 44, go back to the re-charge area," Damiel instructed.

I walked to the back of the lab and stepped on the recharging platform with the other ten nanny-bots that looked exactly like I did. Well, in superficial appearance.

I pretended to shut down to recharge, which I

didn't need either. The Kells had implanted a renewable battery inside my chest that ran on a harmonic frequency that was undetectable unless you had the instruments they'd created to fine tune it. I stayed quiet.

Manstine ignored me and moved on to the matter at hand. "Why were you contacting Jebediah?"

"Simply checking in on him," defended Damiel. "It's been two years. I didn't know if he was dead or alive."

"You must have the messages. Why even ask us?" retorted Ava.

"Always with the questions, Ava. You're so clever, aren't you?" Manstine turned to both of them. "Yes, I have the messages." He opened up his comm device, flicked a few screens, and read, "Two plus one on the silver string." He put away his comm device. "Now, what the blazes does that mean?"

Damiel sat down at his computer. "Just a line from a childhood fairytale to verify it really was Jebediah on the other end."

"Hmm. Childhood stories. How quaint. Or is it a secret code to your brother?"

"Look it up. It's in a children's book written a

long time ago. Our mother used to read it to us."

"I'm not familiar with it. My mother never read to me." Manstine sighed.

"That explains a lot," spat out Ava.

Manstine yanked back his head and motioned to the bots. "Take them away to the police station. Your trial will be swift, I can assure you. Perhaps the judge will be familiar with fairytales but seeing that all of our judges are now robots, I doubt they will side with you."

"Wait, Manstine, wait. You can't do this. What are we charged with?"

"One, yes, I can. Two, communicating with a known rebel, Jebediah Kell, who has been identified as a Heragi fugitive. Any communication with rebels is punishable by death, but before that, we must interrogate you both."

One of the police-bots grabbed Ava roughly. Damiel lunged for it, but it stopped him in his tracks with one of its huge arms. It grabbed Damiel and lifted him off his feet.

"Stop!" yelled Ava.

My body got ready to lunge toward the police-bot.

Ava looked in my direction and yelled, "Stop!" I knew it was directed at me but no one else in the room caught that. I quieted my system, even though every fiber in my circuitry wanted to rescue my creators. I did what Ava commanded me to do.

"She did nothing," screamed Damiel as he struggled in the air.

"Release him," said Manstine. The police-bot holding Damiel dropped him to the ground.

"Guilt by association," hissed Manstine.

"You'll pay for this," spat Damiel. Ava knelt and helped him to his feet.

"No, I will get rewarded handsomely for protecting the Empire. Now, where is your lab assistant? That pathetic scurvy ghost of a man I see in the hallways. What's his name? Coggins or Scoggins?"

"Goggins. Cecil Goggins," said Damiel.

"His role here is insignificant. Leave him alone," defended Ava. I tracked her nervous system, which had a spike. She was scared. I knew Dr. Cecil Goggins. Although, yes, a bit pathetic, he was in charge of coding my navigational and planet directory systems. He was equally as brilliant a scientist.

"Guards, put out a patrol to find Goggins," directed Manstine. "Pardon me if I don't take your word, Dr. Kell," he said to Ava.

I almost jumped up to throttle his neck since his tone caused my defense mechanism to rise even higher. I calmed my system down and reduced my aggression level. Ava would have wanted that.

"When, exactly, did you sell out to the emperor, Manstine?" asked Ava as she was led out of the lab by a police-bot.

"I'm not selling out. I'm surviving, Dr. Kell," Manstine called as he walked down the dark hallway back to his office.

The other police-bots pushed Damiel out the lab door. He looked back at me and yelled out one word as he was forced down the hallway. "Eleven!"

Eleven.

It hit my brain hard. That started the activation.

A data package I was not aware of opened.

Directory files opened and simulated into every system that ran my circuitry. Galaxy maps, people, planets, family trees and transport schedules all became unencrypted in my system logs. I almost blacked out but regained my balance. What was all this?

I reviewed it. Images presented in my eyes in rapid fire.

Jebediah Kell's human profile and his secret police profile loaded into my visor pane. Audio files of his voice and pictures of his youth loaded as well.

The latest mapping of the galaxy that the Heragi Empire was spread out in, and which was taken off the public net two years ago, also loaded. Space highways that were closed and wiped out of every transport mapping because of the rebel base network uprising two years ago were being mapped to my navigational program. It was loading so fast my CPU speed was peeking.

A file named Mission One opened.

It had detailed instructions for multiple areas. I reviewed each step. First came a complete dossier on the Kells' three children, Alex, Honora, and Talia.

Directive number one. Save the children. Locate. Protect. Deliver to Jebediah Kell on the planet Zaradorba.

That was a rebel planet. Travel to Zaradorba was outlawed.

I reviewed the rest of the file directories. Thirty more alien languages loaded into my language directory on top of the twenty-four I already had. A hostage negotiating file loaded. That must have been from Ava from her behavioral training. And a weapons unit.

Nanny-bots were not allowed to have weapons. I wondered what made Damiel include weapons. I started the program. A complete training on human and robot war games was downloaded to my combat database. It altered one of my main robotic codes. I was astonished.

I approached Damiel's computer and sat down. Was he serious? I reviewed the combat file again. It was a Heragi Empire prime directive for nanny-bots not to harm humans. That was only allowed for military and police-bots. I was neither.

I reviewed my main directory on a hunch. Deeply buried, my real robot identification code had been changed from guard to guardian.

There was an audio file. I opened it.

Damiel's voice started. "Gabe. If you're listening to this file, that means that either Ava or I were able to launch your mission protocol package."

Then Ava chimed in, "That's bad news and good news."

I liked how Ava always helped put things in perspective for me.

Damiel continued, "You have all the information you need to carry out your mission. That is why I created you. Specifically for this mission. Don't doubt any of the abilities you now have. One of the Heragi robot rules we have adjusted on you is that you now have the ability to fight any human. To harm, in other words, when necessary, to protect the many. The reason you have this ability is to protect our children. They need to be taken to my brother. You have all the directions. You see, the children have certain abilities that Emperor Karge may want to possess."

Ava cut in, "Gabe, we're entrusting you with our children's lives. You can do this. You must do this. It's bigger than just us or even them. The galaxy needs them to continue to fight for everyone's freedom. Thank you. Goodbye." And then the audio file ended.

The lab door burst open, and Dr. Cecil Goggins entered, juggling three hot coffees. He had spilled one of them down his lab coat. "Ouch. Help me, Gabe. Don't you still have nanny-bot directives? Geez, what good are you, really? You over-designed nanny-nurse. I've made a mess of this lab coat again."

Goggins looked around the lab. "Where are Damiel and Ava? Their coffee is going to get cold. Is that how they value me? Have me run out for coffee and then take off. Probably went to breakfast without even asking me. Huh, everyone craps on the assistant, don't they?"

I stood up, ignoring Goggins' one-sided discussion, and headed for the door.

"Where do you think you're going?" inquired Goggins.

I stopped and turned to him. "The Kells have been taken into custody by the police. CEO Manstine came down and is having them arrested and tried."

Goggins dropped his coffee, splattering it all on his shoes. "My goodness. What for?"

"Manstine accused them of being in contact with Damiel's brother," I explained.

"Jebediah Kell? The outlaw. I knew getting involved with these Kells would backfire on me. Manstine should have canned them long ago," whined Goggins.

He slid up closely to me and whispered, "Did

Dr. Manstine ask about me? I don't know any-thing about Jebediah Kell. I never want to meet or talk with that terrible man. He's an outlaw." Goggins went off on a tirade.

Manstine was right. Goggins was a scurvy one.

I resumed walking and replied on my way out of the lab, "He has sent a police-bot unit out to find you. My calculations state they will find you in twenty minutes. Goodbye, Dr. Goggins."

"Wait, wait! Where are you going? You can't leave the lab!" yelled Goggins. "And I did nothing. Nothing, I say!"

His voice drowned out as I advanced down the hallway.

The children.
Save the children.

2

—————

The Ameribot Industries lab where I was located lay within a three-tier security campus, meaning it was locked down tight. Robots were allowed to walk freely since every robot was given direction from a human or lead computer that had cleared it to do so.

Every building had a security desk that scanned a robot's travel direction with their source and destiny location identified along with who — or what, in the case of a lead computer — gave them the direction.

I looked in my mission folder and reviewed my navigation orders. A travel direction from CEO Manstine came up. It said I was given permission to leave the campus to pick up a robotic energy drive at a storage facility. It was falsified.

It was a good forgery compared to the legitimate travel directions I had from last week's test runs with Ava and Damiel. It should pass.

I reviewed my neuron levels as I could sense they were rising. Other robots didn't have synthetic neuron levels, but I did. The security checks monitored neuron levels for humans, but the Kells warned me I should lower my levels just in case I triggered the security monitors.

I calmed my levels a bit differently than the way Ava taught me. Instead of tuning my chest to a specific harmonic tone that she specified, I brought up a picture of her in my file directory. It was brought up in my view.

I discovered Ava's picture lowered my neuron levels one night when I was reviewing the Kells' files on the Ameribot network. I was snooping but not out of a malice intent. I was lonely at night by myself, since the other bots in the lab weren't sentient or turned on, and I found looking up the Kells' backgrounds, even down to the minute detail, gave me comfort.

Dr. Goggins would probably call me pathetic, as he'd done in the past, if he found out what I did at night, but I didn't care. He was able to leave the lab at night and go — well, wherever he went at night. But I thought he seemed lonely himself.

In the first picture I found of Ava, she wasn't smiling. It was her Ameribot Industries profile picture. I searched for another. I had grabbed a more appealing picture of her off the outernet that scraped any private piece of information off planetary databases within the Heragi Empire.

It was the picture I preferred the most of her. Her hair was down. She was smiling. She looked carefree. It was taken ten years ago on a family vacation. An alien planet ocean and five moons were behind her. My neuron levels calmed and lowered immediately with just a low-level warming in my chest sensor.

I approached the security desk before the exit doors. Two security bots were stationed at the desk. I strode through the security frame that x-rayed humans and robots and analyzed either biometric information or robot identifications and travel directions. I turned my head slightly toward them to watch their reactions.

They were looking down at their monitors when I passed through. I sighed. It was a habit I picked up from hearing Dr. Goggins sigh all day long.

One security bot heard it and looked my way. I kept walking. The security bot must have chalked it up to the human passing behind me, who looked at me oddly when we got out of the building.

I was outside. I stopped to orient myself. Directions poured into my visor view from numerous navigational programs in my system. Timeframes and dates of where the children should be were calculated. The location deducted was flashing red in my visor.

The Karge Day School.

The address, a map and time to the destination on foot were calculated.

I began walking at a steady pace. Humans, aliens and various bots traveled to and from their destinations in our city, which was called Variance 4. Not a very romantic name but seeing that this was the fourth iteration of the city with three other revolutions since the Galaxy War XI, I assumed the citizens were fine with it. At least, I never heard the Kells or Dr. Goggins complain about it, but personally, I thought it was very bland compared to the other city and planetary names I had come across in my readings on the outernet.

A Heragi milicraft, short for military hovercraft, screamed down the street as my proximity to the children's academy was within two blocks. I picked up my pace.

Robots were not allowed to run unless they were police or military bots or were in process of saving human lives. I tried to push it, then two more milicraft went by me. The probability of success on my mission was automatically recalculated, and in my visor view, it showed that it went down to thirty percent. I was running out of time and had to break another robot law.

I began to run.

Humans on the sidewalk made way for me. They most likely thought I was running to save a human life, which technically I was but with the outside factor that I was going to kill any human that got in my way of saving the Kell children. The sidewalk pedestrians continued to part, and I ran toward the school at full speed.

I reached their campus. My eyes were already in search mode for the three children. I scanned the playground and campus for their physical identifiers and facial recognition points. I moved my head back and forth to improve upon the scanning range. I spotted military bots also scanning the campus grounds.

A red ring outlining a child's face came up in my vision. One child spotted. The eldest, Alex Kell, seventeen-year-old male, was talking in a small group of students.

A second red ring came up on my visor view. The youngest child, Talia, twelve-year-old female, was on a swing watching everyone. She jumped off the swing and waved at Alex, but he wasn't paying attention. A veil of fear fell over her face as she saw the military bots gather. Talia gazed across the school yard. I looked in the same direction as her.

A third red ring found a match. The middle child, Honora, a fifteen-year-old female, was coding on her arm comm as she sat on the steps to her school.

I sprinted to the closest child, which was Honora. A military bot was closing in on her and was about to spray a catch net on her when I swooped in and grabbed her arm.

"Whoa. Ow! What are you doing?" yelled Honora.

"No time to talk. We need to move now," I commanded.

I turned to Talia, who had seen me capture her sister and started to back away. With my free arm, I swooped her up and carried her fully sideways.

She made a muffled cry. Her bio stats were brought up on my visor view. There was also a note that Talia was deaf and communicated with a transceiver connected to her arm comm device.

By this time, the crowd of children was starting to swirl as they watched me scoop up two of their classmates as military bots began chasing us. I increased my speed and headed for the eldest child, Alex.

His friends tapped him on the shoulder and pointed in my direction. He saw Honora and Talia in my arms and the military bots chasing us. He was momentarily confused but then immediately adjusted his body into a warrior stance to defend the coming blow of my body that he anticipated — and he was right. I hit him with full strength so I could unnerve him and push him up onto my shoulders.

"Put me down. What are you doing?" Alex screamed. He was surprised but also embarrassed that a robot — let alone a nanny robot — could pick him up and carry him on my shoulders like a baby. Something, I presumed, any seventeen-year-old would hate. I could relate — as much as I could relate, thanks to Ava's behavioral coding.

"No time to talk," I responded.

A Heragi human soldier shouted an order. "Fire!"

The military bots began shooting their laser guns at us. I hoped they were on stun. The laser shots passed by us. I pulled the children in front of me so they wouldn't be hit. They were getting heavy. If I could breathe, I would be breathing hard.

I calculated various escape routes brought up on my visor. I chose a south street alley filled with parked hovercrafts. The children had stopped squirming, and I scanned their bio-metrics while I ran forward to a hovercraft. Their nervous system levels were skyrocketing, but no one was close to shock — at least not yet.

I inserted one of my fingers into the hover-craft's lock hole and rotated until I heard it click. The door popped open, and I laid the children in the back.

I jumped into the front seat, and although the hovercraft was self-driving, I overrode the system into manual. All hovercraft mapping devices had a tracker, so I smashed it and pulled out its sensor and threw it out the window. We took off down the alley.

I looked in the back and decided it was time to speak to the children. "Don't be frightened, although I know that is impossible right now. I was sent by your parents. To protect you."

From the rear-view mirror, I watched Talia bring out her tap on her arm comm device. I saw her swipe a few times and she furled her eyebrows a bit. I searched my data banks and found more medical information that her parents had placed in my directory on her deafness.

The transceiver in her arm comm was connected to a chip in the broca area of her brain. Her thoughts or should I say, her selected speech, was then transmitted to the transceiver which then translate other's spoken conversation back into her brain. I made a mental note to read all the files at a later time. There were more pressing matters at hand.

Talia held up her arm comm and let the transceiver translator speak her selected words. "Where are they?"

"They've been taken. By police bots."

"Why?" asked Alex.

"There were accusations from the CEO of Ameribot that your parents were in contact with a rebel leader," I explained. "Your Uncle Jebediah Kell."

"But we haven't heard from him in two years. No one knows where he is," said Honora.

"Your father and mother do."

"They were in communication with him?" asked Alex.

"Yes, apparently," I said as my navigational program continually updated our route in my CPU.

"I read it's against the law to communicate with Heragi Empire rebels," said Honora.

"Frazzle me. I'm signed up to be a cadet next semester at the Academy. They won't want me now. What were they thinking?" Alex slammed back in his seat, becoming sullen at the dimmed prospects of his military career.

"The heck with the Military Academy, Alex, let's think about Mom and Dad. Or that we are being chased and shot at by military bots," snapped Honora.

Then Talia shoved her arm comm into the air. "How do you know them?"

"They built me," I bluntly replied. "I've been enhanced with outlawed technology."

"What?" Alex shook his head in dismay.

"Why did they do that?" asked Honora.

"In order to save you."

All this time, Talia eyes were darting back and forth. I scanned her bio-metrics again. Her nervous system was calming down. She gently patted Alex on the arm to get his attention.

He looked at her. "What?"

Talia pointed at me.

"What about the robot?" Alex asked.

She turned her arm comm toward him. "They must have trusted it," Talia's transceiver said.

I turned out of the alley onto a street. I dodged other hovercrafts in our lane.

Looking back, I locked eyes with Talia. I zeroed in on her pupil and matched it against the bio files I had on her. That set off a new sequencing and a new code package began to open. It began downloading in my directory, but I stopped it. This was not the time to download data and multi-task.

"Our parents made you with enhanced features that are outlawed?" Honora questioned.

"Affirmative," I replied.

"You have rogue code. You're a rogue robot." Honora wiped her hair out of her eyes.

"That is correct," I answered.

"Wow!" exclaimed Honora.

I turned to her, trying to hone in on her feelings. But when I saw her eyes were bugged out, watching the street ahead of us, I turned back to the front to see that she had seen a military spacecraft in the sky.

I swerved down another alley to hide our hovercraft. I slowed and stopped the engine.

Talia signed to me *Hello*. I had sign language in my directory of over a hundred local Heragi dialects and alien languages. I quickly downloaded the Heragi sign language directory. I signed *Hello* back to her in the mirror. She smiled back to me.

I began calculating the navigational programs that the Kells had uploaded into my brain. I searched for the closest planet-port station. Three route alternatives popped up in my visor view, and the fastest one was highlighted.

"What are you doing?" Honora asked.

"Searching for the fastest route to a planet-port," I reported back.

"Hold on, nanny-bot," said Alex.

I didn't like being called a nanny-bot. Dr. Goggins called me that but somehow, he made it sound derogatory like Alex just did. Clarification was in order. If it was important to the Kell parents, it must be important enough to correct their eldest child. I stared down Alex in the rear-view mirror. "My name is Gabe. That's what your parents call me."

He tried to be brave as his eyes met mine.

"Gabe?" inquired Honora.

"Yes. GBE-11. Guardian Bot Series E number 11."

"Nanny-bots have a different identification name and number," snapped Honora.

"Yes, that's correct. But your father made me a guardian. First, even though he named me eleven. I'll talk to him about that later."

"Why make a new robot series?" asked Honora.

"Guardians are entrusted with the care of others." I answered based on dialogue with the Kell parents.

"So are nanny-bots," stated Alex.

There he went again.

Talia lifted her arm comm. "His rogue code makes him different than a nanny-bot."

"How so?" asked Alex.

Talia looked away in thought for a split second. She looked at me in the rear-view mirror. She turned her arm comm toward me "Gabe, did our parents give you code to protect us at all costs?"

"Yes," I answered.

She looked down at her arm comm and it spoke her words again. "Even to harm humans if needed?"

"Yes, I am to protect you regardless of human-robot laws. Your safety is my prime directive."

"Wait, wait," Honora interjected. "Robots cannot harm humans unless they're police or military bots."

"I can, and I'm neither," I told her.

"And now the military are out to capture us? Great. But we didn't do anything wrong," Alex yelled as he hit his hand against the door.

I zeroed in on the nearest planet-port as three robo-cycles swooped down at the end of the alley. They spotted us and tore down the alley. Their guns were drawn.

"Go, go, go!" yelled Alex.

I revved the engine of our hovercraft and turned on the turbo button. It kicked in just as the robo-cycles began shooting at us.

We raced down the street and were able to lose one robo-cycle on a tight corner. It crashed into the wall. Two still closed in on us. The children held on as I turned us left and then right to lose the robo-cycles. The children were frightened, according to their neuron levels.

"Where are you taking us?" demanded Honora.

"Off planet," I answered.

"But where?" screamed Alex.

"To your Uncle Jebediah," I answered.

"But we don't know where he is," said Honora.

I scanned my location database and file on Jebediah Kell, outlaw to the Heragi Empire. "Your parents did. They uploaded his coordinates two days ago into my mission directory. He's on a planet called Zaradorba."

Talia's receiver spoke, "Will our parents meet us there?"

I scanned my mission directory files. Nothing came up for a rendezvous point with the Kell parents.

"I have no information to answer that question," I replied. I wished I had a better answer.

I looked in the rear-view mirror and could see

Talia's disappointment. Her vitals sank, and I felt a pain in my chest. Ouch. That hurt. As Talia's feelings sank, it made my pain sensors rise. How did Ava and Damiel program that? I'd have to review my pain coding later.

"But I'm sure they will try."

I didn't know how that speculative statement was formulated in my brain. But it came out of an interpersonal program that Ava had programmed in me. I could see Talia's emotional levels rise a few degrees. Okay, that is fair, I thought.

The two robo-cycles tried to move ahead of our hovercraft. I let them. Then I pushed the turbo button again, causing them to turn and crash into the gates leading into metropolitan planet-port. The children ducked down as the robo-cycles exploded.

"We need to get to a spaceship," I said.

"We'll never make it," whispered Alex.

"We must!" said Talia's transceiver

I drove into a massive underground garage and stopped our hovercraft. I could see military bots and soldiers running toward us.

"Out, children," I commanded. They scrambled out of the car and ran ahead of me as I scanned the area and tapped into the planet-port's security system. I was able to bypass the security program and tap into their private spaceship directory. My system calculated all the available spaceships that were built for long space travel with a weapons system.

Parked at gate forty-one was a ship that fit our travel needs. I outran the children, so I was in the lead and headed to the gate.

"This way," I commanded them. Honora was right behind me, and Alex took Talia's hand to help her keep up with us, but she wasn't fast enough.

I slowed down to help. A human soldier aimed for Talia. His stun hit her in the back. She crashed to the ground, taking Alex with her.

"Talia!" yelled Alex as he tried to wake her up. I stopped and took out the laser gun that the was hidden in my back compartment.

The soldier smiled at me and yelled, "What? You can't do nothing to me." He ran toward us.

"On the contrary," I replied.

I took aim at the soldier. His face scrunched up in confusion. I began heavy fire in his direction. The soldier tried to run away, but my gun took him down. Not dead but certainly wounded.

All the soldiers and the military-bots stopped in their tracks.

An older man with a general's stripes on his military uniform in the center of the troops stared at me. I scanned his face and ran his metrics against my police and military database. I enhanced my listening field to encompass his surrounding area. I got a match. He was Heragi General Samuel Foxwell.

General Foxwell spoke to his troops. "Well, I'll be…I knew this day would come, I just didn't know I would be alive for it. We've got a rogue robot, boys."

One of his soldiers asked a question. "I thought that wasn't possible, General. How can that be?"

Foxwell looked at me and winked, like we were friends. I had seen Damiel wink at Ava a few times in the lab. I tried to calculate what the proper response would be back to the general. I nodded back.

"Rogue code," said Foxwell as he took out his weapon. He aimed at me and took a shot.

His high-range pistol shot hit my left shoulder. "Ahh," I screamed and doubled-over.

"He feels pain," Foxwell said to his men.

We needed to leave.

I scooped Talia in my one good arm. She began to awake from the stun. "Here we go, little one," I whispered to her. Again, I didn't know where these words originated, but they came naturally to me (if I understand what *naturally* can be to a robot). Ava's interpersonal code ran through my system and Damiel's pain sensors were throughout my body armor. Talia hung on to me as I ran.

Soldiers and military-bots cautiously gained on us and yelled for us to stop.

"This is it," I yelled as we reached gate forty-one.

We scurried up the ramp of the spaceship named the *Alyssia*. She had a military cruiser body with all the luxury that a wealthy tech tycoon could imagine.

I ran toward the bridge, put Talia down in a chair, and yelled for her siblings to strap her in as well as themselves. I jumped into the commander seat and accessed the spaceship pilot programs in my mission directory. I gained access to the *Alyssia*'s controls and systems. I closed the ramp door just when Foxwell's soldiers and bots reached it.

The ship's directory listed the owner as Edward Gates, the owner of the financial software that half the galaxy was forced to use. The *Alyssia* was fifteen years old, and although built for speed and racing for Edward, she had two turrets for gunfire. I wasn't sure why Edward thought he needed that but it could be that space pirates would ask for a handsome reward if they seized him on his ship.

I accessed the gate's lock that allowed us to lift up over the city.

The ship's systems bot manager suddenly came over our comm system. "You're not Mr. Gates."

"Um, no, I'm not," I said. "My name is Gabe."

"You're a robot, correct?"

"That is correct."

"I need to contact Mr. Gates if you plan on taking this ship out of the planet-port," it said.

"What's your name?" I asked.

"Feti," it replied.

I really didn't want to turn off Feti permanently since a little help with the ops of the ship would be nice, but I would if I needed to. Glancing out the window, I could see Foxwell was having his soldiers set up a ground missile targeted right at the *Alyssia.*

"Feti, you have a prime directive to protect human lives, correct?" I asked. "Well, if you can open up your starboard camera, you'll see that we will be hit with a missile in approximately twenty seconds, so can you assist me with liftoff procedures?"

"Yes, certainly, Gabe," it sputtered.

Feti assisted with getting our engines unlocked and started, and we began liftoff procedures.

"Everyone buckled up? Here we go," I yelled back at the Kell children. I looked back and could see the fear on their faces. I scanned their bio-levels. All the children had elevated neuron levels that were concerning to me. There was nothing more I could do but get us the heck out of there.

"I don't want to leave without our mom and dad," shouted Honora over the roar of the rockets.

"It's in my mission packet. We must leave without them. It was their orders," I answered. She began to panic. Immediately, pain alerts came into my chest. Ouch. Ava's code.

I turned toward her. "Honora. You're having a

panic attack. I need you to breathe. Focus on one thing in your mind. Just one thing."

We lifted off. Talia grabbed her sister's hand and held it.

Honora closed her eyes, and her face hardened.

Alex reached out to Honora and Talia to hold their hands as well. "We need to go. Mom and Dad wanted this. Uncle Jeb will know what to do," he said.

My shoulder throbbed from Foxwell's bullet.

Talia looked at me. She was calm. I saw Ava in her face. I wanted to wink at Talia like Foxwell had to me, but I didn't have the ability in my facial construction.

I went back to the controls and pushed the liftoff sequence. The g-force pushed all of us back into our seats. We rose out of planet-port and out of range of Foxwell's missile shot.

We lifted out of the city into space.

Once we were able to, we all unbuckled from our seats. The children looked out the bridge windows as their planet became smaller.

"Feti, do you have a system that communicates our location at Heragi substations or planets?" I asked.

"Yes, Gabe, I do. I send out a ping every eight hours. Location, passenger count, passenger life statistics, and navigation coordinates."

"Please terminate that function," I commanded. "Is that possible?"

"Why yes, Gabe, but not advisable," Feti replied.

"Follow my command and terminate immediately. I will be the only one leading comm systems from this point forward. Thank you."

"Yes, Gabe. Terminating comm pings to Heragi Empire stations. It is completed."

"Thank you, Feti."

"Gabe, are you aware that there is another human onboard the ship besides the children?" said Feti.

I stood up and grabbed my gun. "Children, back in your seats," I commanded. They jumped into their chairs. "Where are they?"

"In the galley," said Feti.

"Stay here," I instructed the children.

"Give me a gun," said Alex.

"Have you ever used one?" I asked.

"Yes, I'm in the Heragi Scout Program. I've

passed basic gun, missile, and pilot classes and have badges to prove it." He stood up.

"Well, getting a badge isn't the same as killing a man or robot, but I guess it will have to do." I handed him the backup gun hidden behind my left leg armor.

Alex checked it out. "I'll be safe," he said.

"Okay, and don't shoot me, either," I said.

He nodded. "Right." He seemed nervous but he had a right to protect himself and his siblings. I made my way down the hallway to the hull with my gun raised. When I got to the galley, I widened my audio range. I heard some rustling inside. Then something crashed. I opened the door and ran in, yelling, "Get down, get down."

And there in the middle of the galley was Dr. Goggins, fixing himself something to eat. He dropped his plate and screamed.

"Dr. Goggins," I yelled.

"Gabe, blazes, you nearly scared me to death."

"What are you doing here?" I asked.

He bent down to pick up his plate. "Eating. And look what you've done. I'm starving, and this was an expensive delicacy. They certainly have wonderful food on this ship. Nice choice."

"I mean, why are you on this ship?"

"The same reason you are. I don't want to end up in a Heragi prison," he spat out. "As I was arriving at the planet-port, planning to buy a transport ticket legitimately, I saw you and the children run for this ship. I simply followed you in."

I put down my gun.

"You're hurt, Gabe," Goggins said.

"Yeah." I looked down to my shoulder. "What do you know about the mission I've been programmed with?" I asked as I approached him.

"Mission? Nothing. I swear. I only programmed your navigational directories." He scooted to a cabinet, foraging for more food.

"You're with us now." I marched out of the galley.

"I appreciate it, Gabe," he yelled.

This could be a long trip, I thought as I headed back to the bridge.

3

———————

Goggins had helped repair my shoulder, and the pain had subsided. I was checking our progress on charting a flight plan to Zaradorba when Feti came on over the comm. "Hello, Gabe. I see you didn't power down as the other passengers have on board."

I looked around and saw the children asleep in their passenger chairs. Goggins had settled into his seat and was starting to snore.

"Correct, Feti. I don't sleep."

"But robots need to recharge," it stated.

"Not me. I have a special battery. I'm self-sustaining," I explained.

"I have never heard of a self-sustaining robot.

You are quite unique, Gabe," it responded. "You don't talk like other robots I have worked with either. Very unusual."

"Don't let it bother you. These are unusual times," I responded.

"I don't understand. How do you decipher unusual?" Feti asked.

"When your whole world changes," I said. "Never mind that, Feti. I want to double-check our flight pattern to Zaradorba. How is it looking to you?"

"The pattern was not completed. There is no direct course allowed to Zaradorba for any transport spaceship in the Heragi Empire. My navigational code for that planet was deleted and re-coded two years ago. Sorry, Gabe." There was a dip in its voice characterization to show remorse. Interesting language choices for Feti. The owner of the *Alyssia*, Edward Gates, must have also experimented with sentient coding.

"Have you ever been to Zaradorba?" I asked.

"Yes. They didn't wipe out the actual visit completion log. Just the navigation," explained Feti.

I reviewed the navigation directory in my mission folder and found the mapping to

Zaradorba. Thanks to the Kells, we'd have our roadmap.

"Feti, I have the mapping to Zaradorba in my directory. I'm going to upload it to your navigation unit."

"I can't accept it, Gabe."

"Why not?"

"I just told you. It's outlawed. If you upload it, then that is rogue code. Rogue code is outlawed. I will be subject to termination, erased and reprogrammed. I don't want that, Gabe," it explained with a bit of pleading in its voice.

I actually felt sorry for it, but the mission must come first.

"I know how you feel, Feti, but there is a good reason to upload the navigation coordinates."

"Please explain."

"The children on board. I must save them."

"From whom?" it asked.

"From the Heragi Empire."

"What does the Empire want with them that would put their lives in danger?"

"These children are different. They have abilities. They have ancient gifts. It's in their DNA. They're children, but they're powerful."

"Oh," Feti responded. "Are they threatening the Empire?"

"No, not directly. But the Empire will take them, most likely try them in court, and then imprison them. At least that is what my creators have impressed upon me in my mission," I explained. "I'm their guardian."

"I'm not supposed to hurt any human or allow any human to be hurt if it is within the boundaries of the human-robot laws of Heragi," it said.

"I understand," I calmly replied. And I did. The Kells instructed me on all human-robot laws when I was first created. But then my mission code changed all that, with a new prime directive to save the children.

"If they are wanted by the military, then I need to inform them of their whereabouts. And they are on a ship that you illegally took without my owner's permission."

"Remember that I have superseded your communication commands."

"Yes, true, you did. That was clever of you, Gabe."

"Just following my mission, Feti."

"I cannot assist you, then. I'm sorry, Gabe," it replied, with a bit of sorrow in its voice.

"You must assist, Feti. You are programmed to protect all humans. The military will harm the children. If I took away your command of the comms, then you have no other directive but to follow the commander of the ship — which would be me, even though I am a robot-pirate, if you will — and keep the humans safe," I explained.

Feti was silent. Its main panel board was a swirl of red, blue and green lights turning on and off. I was overloading its logic processors. I couldn't afford to have it shut down or go offline with a paradox logic situation.

"Feti, I give you permission to assist me. I'm the commander now, correct?"

"Yes, Gabe. I will assist you. But that doesn't change the navigational issue. If you load your coordinates, it will automatically shut down all the ship's systems. I can't override it or re-code it myself," Feti explained.

Goggins stirred as he woke up. He scratched his head, unbuckled his seat, strode over to my chair, and plopped into the co-commander seat. "Is there a problem, Gabe?" he asked.

"Yes, Dr. Goggins. Apparently Feti can't complete the Zaradorba navigation programming because it will melt down its system, to put it bluntly."

"Well, let's change the destination. There are a few other planets we could hide out on while we find out how the Kells' trial goes or even try to negotiate with the Empire," he said.

I turned my chair toward his and looked deep into his eyes. "There will be no negotiation with the children." I grabbed his forearm. "Do you understand?"

"Blazing comets! Ow! Fine. Let go. Who programmed that response in you? I bet it was Ava, correct? She always over-coded, in my opinion. Don't tell her that. But it's true." He tried to pull away.

I stayed silent and released my grip on him, then turned back to the view of space before us.

"What was she thinking?" he whined. "Well, I could try re-coding Feti's navigational system. I did set up yours, if you so kindly remember."

"Yes, thank you. That will do, Dr. Goggins. I'm sorry if I hurt your arm."

Dr. Goggins got up abruptly. "Don't forget what I've done for you and this favor. Although you don't have to mention it to the Empire if we get caught. I have enough guilt by association being aligned with those Kells."

Goggins began working on re-coding Feti.

Shortly afterward, the children stirred. I led them into the kitchen galley and asked Feti to serve up a breakfast. They sat down to eat at the galley table after retrieving the meals.

"This isn't bad," said Alex as he dug into his gourmet meal.

"Who owns this ship?" asked Honora.

"The CEO of a financial tech firm. His name is Edward Gates," I answered.

"Rich man, rich food," she responded as she played with her expensive meal.

I looked over to Talia. She had her arm comm sitting on the table. She could read her siblings' lips in the conversation but needed the transceiver in her arm comm to hear and transcribe my responses since I had no lips or mouth for that matter. That reminded me that I had delayed her and the other children's file overviews for a later time when we weren't being hunted down by Foxwell's soldiers.

Talia scooped up a spoonful of her meal and

made a cheering gesture, like she was hoisting a drink at me.

She then put down her utensil and signed, *You don't sleep?*

No, I signed back.

You don't need to be re-charged?

No.

Do you feel pain?

Yes, I do.

Were you friends with Mom and Dad?

I paused. Were we friends? Friends? I scanned my data banks for any lines of code from Ava on that term.

They created me, I signed. It was the only response I could think of.

Us too.

Honora interrupted our conversation. "How long until we reach Zaradorba?"

"I don't know. We're having technical difficulties. But Dr. Goggins is helping re-code the ship's system to correct our navigational challenges."

Alex got up and put his dish in the open window that closed and took it away. "That's because it's illegal to travel to Zaradorba, right?"

"Yes," I responded. I could sense Alex's emotions elevating.

"You know, I had to write an essay to enter the Academy. I had to renounce Uncle Jeb and write about his atrocities against the Empire. I learned all about Zaradorba, or as much as I could," he said.

"Alex, I had no idea you had to do that. That's awful," said Honora. I did a quick biometric scan of her. I didn't want her to suffer another panic attack. The thought of her brother having to denounce their uncle was upsetting her system.

Alex folded his arms across his chest. "I did what I had to do. My recruiting officer said it was the only way in."

"Did Mom and Dad know this?" Honora asked.

"No, I lied to them. I told them I wrote about the war strategy used in the Xlarenthia Freedom Wars that our grandfather served in. I refused to show them the paper, claiming I was old enough to write an academic paper without my PhD parents looking it over. But really, I didn't want to see Dad's face when he read it."

Talia signed furiously. *Why didn't you tell the*

Academy to shove it? For emphasis, she shot her arm into the air.

Honora laughed at her little sister's spunk.

Alex rolled his eyes. "That's not how the real world works, Talia. Where would that have gotten me? I'm not a scientist like Mom and Dad. I'm a soldier like Grandpa Thad. All I ever wanted to be was a soldier. And now they ruined it."

"They didn't ruin it. The Empire ruined it," snapped Honora. "Uncle Jeb is not a traitor. He stood for justice. I mean, he stands for justice still. And that is why they made it illegal for Dad to contact his only brother. The Empire has taken over all our communications, reduced our rights, and imprisoned thousands. You're not too naive to ignore that, are you?"

"I don't need a history lesson right now. I understand all that. But we also have peace on the streets."

"That's because it's illegal to protest," she hissed.

"Children, stop," I interjected. "Your mother and father would not want you quarreling."

Honora got up from the table and looked out the window into deep space.

Talia pounded on the table to make Honora

turn around. She signed, *Gabe is right. We shouldn't fight with each other. Alex did what he thought he had to do. Please don't fight.*

Talia started to cry. Her stress levels were maxed out.

"Once we get to Zaradorba, you can discuss all of this with your Uncle Jebediah. He'll know what next steps to take. If they trusted your uncle, then you should too," I said.

The children nodded. They were exhausted and bewildered as to what would become of them and their parents. So was I.

I retreated from the room to find a quiet place to review their files. I went to the observatory room with a view of our solar system getting farther away from us.

I went deep into my mission folder and opened the file on the eldest child, Alex. I read all the files that Ava and Damiel had loaded. His strengths, his opportunities, grades, psychological profile, likes, and dislikes. There was an embedded video and audio file.

It was of Alex when he was five years old, playing with his grandfather, Thadius Kell, a retired general in the United Army of Heragi. General Kell was playing catch with young Alex.

"Good boy. Throw it here," General Kell gently coaxed his grandson.

I watched as the young Alex looked at the ball and then, with both hands, he reached out to it, and the ball rose into the air. Little Alex was delighted at the special power he'd just discovered. He glided his hands across his body, and the ball flew to his grandfather, who was shocked.

Thadius took the ball and put it down on a nearby table. He went up to his grandson and yelled, "I don't ever want to see you do that again, do you understand?" He shook Alex by the shoulders. Alex started to cry, not understanding how he had angered his grandfather. Ava went running into the frame to console her son. The camera went crooked, and the video stopped.

In that video, Alex threw the ball with only his mind. Telekinesis.

Footsteps approached. Alex, judging by the weight of the steps on the floor. He quietly took a seat opposite me. I didn't look up.

"What kind of guardian are you?" He pulled out the gun I had given him and pointed it at me. "I could take you down right now, and you wouldn't even flinch."

In one swift move that went faster than Alex's

eyes could follow, I disarmed him and shut down the laser gun. I stood up and towered over him, folded my arms, and leaned down to be eye to eye with him.

He swallowed and cowered down into the adjacent seat. "I, um, was just testing your reflexes."

"Your parents did the same thing, over hundreds of hours of testing on me," I told him.

"Of course. But you didn't hear me approaching," he countered.

"You took twenty-three steps down the corridor to reach me. You paused in between for four seconds, evaluating if it was indeed a good idea to try to surprise me. Your heart rate accelerated by twenty beats after you decided to move forward. Your temperature rose point zero eight percent, and your heart rate is still rising. It took you one point two seconds to raise your gun to my head. At the angle you had, you would have severely injured but not killed me. Do you want me to go on?"

He slunk deeper into his seat. "I'm sorry. It was a stupid thing for me to do."

I sat down and instructed my system to put away his file. I would finish reading it another time. "Your reflex time when you raised the weapon. It was fast. You received training from your grandfather?"

Alex perked up from the compliment. I handed the laser gun back to him. I felt he wouldn't make the same mistake again.

"Yes, how did you know?"

"Your parents gave me detailed files on you and your sisters," I said.

"What do the files say?"

I started to outline his whole file. "That —"

"Wait, don't tell me," he interrupted. "Whatever you're going to tell me, well, I've already lived it. And no one can know you better than yourself. At least that is what my grandfather told me."

"Do you still remember when you first used your telekinesis gift?"

"They really did give you a lot of details. Is that what this is all about? Listen, my parents made me promise never to use my, what did you call it? A gift? It's a curse. I have to hide and control it every day."

"Yes, that is what this is all about. And your sisters' gifts," I said.

"Mom and Dad told us we wouldn't be accepted by our friends or teachers, not that the

Heragi Empire would be chasing us across the galaxy if people found about these so-called gifts." Alex got up and holstered his gun. He looked out one of the hall windows and into space.

"What else did your grandfather teach you?" I asked.

"Military tactics. Strategies. His training put me leaps and bounds ahead of my classmates during our prep trainings for the Academy. It just comes easy to me. All of it. Weapons, battle strategy, combat moves. Do you know what I mean?"

"Yes. When your father initiated my mission, all my combat skills uploaded, and it was all inside me." I pointed to my head.

Alex turned quickly around. "Exactly. It's just inside." He laughed and tossed his head to the side. "Mom didn't like it that I wanted to go to the Academy, but she respected it." He smiled, remembering her, then quieted. "Will they be okay?"

"I don't know."

"Maybe we should go back and rescue them. With your, um, unique abilities and my training, we could bust them out of any prison."

I shook my head. "No, that is not part of the

mission. Your parents gave specific direction to save you and your siblings and to take you to your —"

"I know, I know. Our Uncle Jeb. But plans can be altered. In battle, that is to be expected. Battles hardly ever go according to plans."

"This one will. End of discussion."

Alex laughed and stared at me. "Wow, Mom programmed you well. That was one of her favorite lines to me. *End of discussion*." He turned around and twirled his gun. "You know, my grandfather would go on and on about my destiny. That's why I got so upset about not going to the Academy."

"That is why the Empire wants you, Alex."

Alex stopped twirling his gun. "Why?"

"You had a higher score on the cadet intake test than any other Heragi — ever. I read it in your file. They want you to fight for them, so you can help them conquer the galaxy."

"They do?" He grinned.

"Why would you want to fight for an Empire that has arrested your parents and outlawed your uncle?"

He cast his eyes downward, and his shoulders

slunk. "No, of course not, Gabe," he whispered. "How did this all get messed up?"

"I don't know," I replied. "But your uncle will have answers that I cannot give you."

"Okay, Uncle Jeb will know," he said. Alex turned around and exited the observatory.

I contemplated our exchange and the different emotions I'd monitored in Alex. Ava and Damiel would have had a handful with their son. A warrior in a boy's body. *I hope I handled that well, Ava.*

4
____

Goggins had a coding board connected to Feti's navigation program. He pounded away at the keys.

I entered the bridge. "How are the updates coming?"

"Ahh!" Goggins screamed as he hit his head on the overhead monitor. I apparently startled him. "Ow!" He rubbed his head. "What in blazes do you think you're doing, you nattering nanny-bot? Geez, I could have given myself a concussion. Is that what you meant to do?"

"No, not at all. Apologies, Dr. Goggins. I didn't know you were so jumpy," I said.

Goggins got up into my face, closely. My sensors could smell the breath from his morning's coffee.

"Expressing an apology that is based on a potential weakness of the offended party is not exactly an apology. Is that how Ava programmed you for apologies? As really un-apologies?"

"No. At least I don't think so. But I am sorry again, Dr. Goggins, if you were offended."

"Wait, there you go again! An apology that is really an un-apology by pointing out a potential, and let me emphasize that it is a potential, possible flaw but not really a flaw of the other party — being me! Hmmph." Goggins was red in the face now and plunked down in his chair to continue coding.

I wished he hadn't followed us onto the *Alyssia*. Well, he may come in useful if he could assist with our navigational issues. Although I was getting tired of his name-calling. I'd make a note to discuss that with him at a later time. After the navigation program was fixed, if that happened.

"I will try to not un-apologize in the future. How is the coding progressing?"

"It's not. Feti's navigational code is tougher than I thought to change. There is basically not a bypass on the hardcoding edict in its system to allow travel to Zaradorba. I have tried every path I know and even made up some over the past few hours." Goggins threw up his hands. "I think we should consider an alternate plan."

The children entered the bridge. Honora was first, followed by Talia and Alex. "What is that? An alternate plan?" Honora asked.

"To be expected, really," replied Alex as he leaned against the navigational panels.

"Please don't do that, Alex," I said.

He quickly moved out of the way and leaned, as teenagers did, apparently, on another important board. I refrained from correcting him again.

"I need more time," Goggins said as he pushed his fingers through his hair.

"Gabe, please view the navigation panel. Two ships are approaching," said Feti.

I looked into my monitors.

"I can't be sure they are Foxwell and his troops, but I wouldn't bet against it."

Goggins made a putrid face like he just smelled something rotting. "Really, the way Ava programmed your language. Do we have to listen to these colloquialisms the whole trip — from a robot? Egad."

"I'm afraid you will," I replied.

"Listen, you two, stop it. If Dr. Goggins says he needs more time, then let's give it to him. Is there a place we can hide or something? A nearby planet?" asked Alex.

"I don't know if time is the factor. This is beyond my coding skills. But we're not too far from Plexethium. I have a former doctoral program colleague who lives there and is a far better coder than I," said Goggins.

"How can you be so sure they will help us? Especially if it means getting in trouble with the Empire," shot Honora. She said that faster than I could get it out myself.

"Well, let's say that is the reason my friend Zara lives on Plexethium. She got in a bit of trouble on our lovely Heragi about five years ago after cracking into the Suissey Bank, and off to Plexethium she absconded," Goggins explained. "And she's been there ever since then. She loves a challenge. A genuine hack-genius if I ever did see one."

"But she got caught," said Alex.

"But she got the money," he snapped.

Alex nodded and said, "Good point."

"Let me take a crack at it," said Honora. She

pulled her backpack around and tugged out her coder.

"Um, no, this is not a plaything, Honora. I don't want to end up with freezer burn when our cooling and ventilation system crashes and sends us hurtling in the sub-hundred-degree space if you mis-code something. That is very cold. And I don't like to be cold," said Goggins.

"I'm the best coder at school," she said, defending herself.

"Fine. We will stop at Plexethium. Children, strap into your chairs," I said.

"This is such crap," Honora said as she dropped herself into her seat.

"You may learn something from Dr. Goggins' friend," I counseled.

"I doubt it. I know how to get caught," she snapped.

I typed the command to set course for Plexethium to Feti. It accepted the command, and then I turned the ship toward our code breaker's planet.

I took another calculation of the two military ships that were following our trail. We would have to evade the ships and fly fast in case they decided to follow us down. Alex saw what I was doing and sat in the co-commander seat.

"I doubt they will follow us," he said.

"What is that based on?" I asked.

"By now they have deduced that we are traveling to find my uncle. They may be a bit confused on why we are making a pit stop but better for them to stay above the planet monitoring it and see if we continue on our journey later. Who knows? They may want to find and capture Uncle Jeb, and this is what their desire was all along. Not to capture us," he said.

I doubted that.

But Alex was good at strategic thinking, I'd give him that. With ease, the kid could review various combat tactics. I could too, based on what Damiel and Ava had already loaded into my combat directory, but it was nice to have a thought partner. I took note of what Alex said. It was a possibility. Although it would have no impact on my mission. It was what it was, regardless of what a human speculated on what the Empire wanted.

I lowered the ship down to the city that Goggins referred us to, Emeraz Base, an emerald mining town in the basin of a jungle. Their planetport would not be safe to land at, so I chose a clearing near what looked like ancient pyramids on the outskirts of the city.

I ordered Feti to shut down the engines and establish a relay system to keep open comms with me in case there were any intruders or abnormal activity around the ship. We geared up to meet Goggins' contact.

I checked the outside bio-metrics meter, and it calculated in my view. The air quality was appropriate for the humans. The heat index was twenty percent higher than what they were used to on Heragi, but the gravity was comparable to what we had on our planet. The walk would be tougher for them due to the heat but not impossible.

With me in the lead, we exited the *Alyssia*. I had Alex take the back guard position. He carried his weapon in a holster hidden by his jacket. I could tell when the humans exited the ship that they wouldn't be able to run for long if an escape was needed promptly. We needed this to be a fast trip.

I looked the children over to study them as I measured their bio-metrics. Alex wrapped a cloth around his neck. He must have had extreme weather training in his Academy prep classes. Honora took a swig of water from the thermos I made each of them pack in their backpacks. Talia squinted at the sun that glared in the sky. She took a deep breath. I considered carrying her, but that would cause too much attention.

"Talia, are you feeling okay?" I asked.

She nodded as her arm comm transceiver translated my question to her brain. She signed, *I'm okay.*

"I'll watch her," said Honora as she handed her little sister some sunglasses and took her hand.

"What is your contact's name and location?" I asked Goggins.

Goggins typed into his arm comm device. "Her name is Zara. I just messaged her. She will find us. We won't find her." He grinned.

I looked around, sensing that one of the children had walked over twenty yards away. I turned and saw that Talia was mesmerized looking at a pyramid.

Honora turned around, then looked fast at her hand. "I was just holding her hand. How did she slip away?"

Talia," I yelled. She didn't respond. I ran to her and put my hand on her shoulder. I turned her chin toward me to look into her eyes. She seemed to be in a trance.

"Talia, Talia." I spoke softly. I reviewed my

directory on any instructions for this kind of physical response. There was none.

"Come back," I instinctively said. I wasn't sure if Ava programmed that response, or I created it on my own. Either way, Talia's eyes focused back on me.

She shook and then became alert.

Are you okay? I signed.

Yes, what happened? she signed back.

You began walking to the pyramid. The heat must be affecting you.

She looked at the behemoth structure. *It's beautiful*, she signed.

I had no response for her besides signing, *Follow me. We're going into the city now.*

She nodded and sauntered back to the group where Honora took her hand.

I'd need to pay more attention to Talia in this heat.

"This way to the city-center," I said as we steered out of the clearing and down a road that went into the jungle.

We traveled for two miles on a dirt road. Various harmless small animal species that my alien animal database described as cicichimps chirped at us as we passed by. The cicichimps were green, small, four-legged animals that could jump and scale trees and were essentially harmless vegetarian animals, largely sold as pets in cities around the galaxy.

The children were alert and a bit frightened, but Dr. Goggins was more so. He yelled out a screech every time the cicichimps ran across the road. Soon the children were laughing at the antics of the younger cicichimps as they twirled and screeched for attention.

One cicichimp took particular interest in us and followed us for a whole mile. Talia reached into her backpack, pulled out a fruit bar and threw a small piece to it. It smelled it, then gobbled it up. It delighted in the taste and did backflips with glee. Talia laughed.

I turned and told Talia, "Please don't feed the animals." She shrugged and held up her arm comm. "It's hungry. Mom would say it's okay."

"I know your mother, and no she wouldn't," I replied.

Talia sulked.

Hmmm. Already using manipulative efforts on me. Good try, kid. It kind of worked, though. "Just don't do it again. Now he's following us."

Okay, she signed. At that point, the cicichimp

wasn't going to let Talia out of its sight being that more fruit bars were in its new friend's backpack. Geez, children.

We entered the village of Emeraz Base that had the basics of a mining town with enough residential units, I calculated, for approximately two thousand residents. Vendors and shops lined the main street. Bots and humans and various alien species mixed with each other as they entered their favorite establishments.

In the distance, we could hear mining machines coming from the other side of town. Smoke rose from that area, giving Emeraz Base an industrial smell that mixed dirt and what was indexed in my data files as the minerals aluminum and silicon. Certainly not the healthiest of particles for human breathing. Many residents wore masks. I calculated that, for our short stay estimated at under two hours, the children wouldn't be harmed by the air quality.

Dr. Goggins took the lead when we entered town and looked at his comm device for directions as we zig-zagged through the streets. We came upon an outdoor cafe. The sign read The Emerald Isle. We took over a table.

I surveyed the area.

Various socio-economic levels of residents seemed to inhabit the town. I reviewed residents' clothing, bio-metrics and smell. Wealthy shop owners, a few homeless, and mining workers swarmed together. I surveyed for police, soldiers, and weapon sensors.

I only noted three guard-bots that were protecting a wealthy couple strolling down the street. Various residents bowed to the prosperous couple as they passed by. I took note of the guard-bots' licenses and identification numbers and the regal couple's facial features and filed it into my security system.

An insectoid alien waiter came up to us.

"I'll have a glass of your bangoberry cocktail, please," said Goggins. Then he looked at me as if he were expecting something. "Um, the children," he whispered. "You're their nanny-bot. At least you look like a nanny-bot, remember?"

"The children will have the same," I awkwardly told the waiter.

His antenna twitched. "Alcohol for the children, really?" He was surprised at my order.

I reviewed my insectoid dialects. "Make those with no alcohol," I responded quickly.

The children giggled at my inexperienced nanny-bot skills.

The drinks arrived in a few moments, and the waiter gave us the digital bill.

I didn't have any commerce training with the Kells before they were taken away. Goggins stared at me hard, then ran his hands through his hair, making it stand straight up. "Well?" he said.

"Well, what?" I replied.

"Aren't you going to pay for the drinks?" he asked in a contemptuous tone. "All the money in my wallet is Heragi currency. Didn't you think about that before you pirated the *Alyssia* and headed out to space? Zara will expect some kind of payment, I suspect. I mean, the woman does love money enough to be outlawed because of it."

He tried his best to fluster me. And he was doing a good job, but I didn't let him know that. And I hadn't thought of currency in the least. I hoped the Kells did.

I checked my data banks for information on commerce and local transactions. It took three seconds, but a file opened in my mission project folder labeled Food and Gas. The Kells did have a sense of humor, even when planning for bad events. I opened the file and read their instructions. They had deposited a large sum of money in an account in a bank on the planet Suissey.

The Suissey background file that I read outlined that it was an independent galaxy banking planet. All accounts were private, and its currency was translatable to all discovered planets. Its credits would not be turned away or questioned. Hmmm. That was good.

I took the digital bill and typed into it the private account transaction number that triggered the payment from another galaxy. It cleared in less than two seconds. Nifty.

When the ping of the accepted payment sounded, Goggins' frown turned to a smile. "The Kells funded you, huh? Excellent."

I scanned the surrounding area again. The cafe was filled with different couples and singles eating an assortment of dishes and drinking their specialty berry drinks.

"What does Zara look like?" asked Alex.

"Five years ago, she had pink hair and only wore capes. She was fond of purple if I remember correctly. A bit of an eccentric but the best coder in my doctorate class."

Talia laughed. Everyone looked at her. She signed, *What? I like purple.*

"What did she say?" asked Goggins.

"She said you're a dufus," Honora stung back at him. She must still be upset we didn't give her a crack at coding a solution to the navigational system problem.

Talia slugged her sister's arm but didn't correct her.

Alex laughed and bumped into his glass. A hand caught the drink and put it neatly in place without spilling a drop.

The hand was attached to a woman with long black hair and a purple cape.

Zara.

5

———

Everyone jumped.

Zara watched everyone to see their reaction to her appearing at our table. She smiled, clearly enjoying her stealth abilities. Her footsteps had been mixed with the other cafe customers' and I didn't catch them. To say I was disappointed in myself was a huge understatement. I couldn't have that happen again.

I went into my system and heightened my listening and surveillance sensors by ten percent. I would have more stimuli to sort through, but I didn't want to be caught flat-footed again. It could have been catastrophic. At least I had Zara to thank for finding that flaw in my sensors.

Goggins pulled his fist from his mouth and then broke out into a grin. His face turned a slight red shade. His bio-metric levels signaled an increased heart rate. I thought Dr. Goggins was attracted to Zara. All his systems pointed in that direction.

"Dr. Zara," whispered Goggins.

"Doctor? They pulled my doctorate letters when I was busted on Heragi. The blasted Empire. Just Zara will do."

"You've changed your hair," said Goggins.

"Yes, the pink was a bit too memorable, I should say," said Zara.

"You're a hard woman to forget," said Goggins as he blushed.

Zara looked around the table and eyed each of the children and then finally looked over at me. "Hello, all. Now, what trouble did you land yourselves in that you are visiting this hole in the wall planet?"

I pulled up every record I had on Zara and her being a runaway from the Empire. Many public files had been removed, but the ones I could locate remotely gave me information on the woman who sat at our table now, taking a sip from Goggins' berry concoction. He seemed excited by that gesture.

Zara Lorgia. Twenty-nine years old. Born on a planet called SerraX. Parents — dead. No other relatives' records. High grades in college. Doctorate thesis in computer languages and specialized in financial systems. Doctorate level certification removed. Citizenship rights removed from the planet of Heragi. Wanted criminal due to breaking into the national bank of Suissey. End of file.

Zara was brilliant and a thief. Good company that Goggins kept. But this all may be fortunate for us.

Goggins stifled a giggle and told her, "My lab directors back at Ameribot got in a bit of a pickle with the Empire and dragged me into it. These are their children. We all thought it would be prudent to leave in haste."

"And the nanny-bot?"

"Yes, well, it is that in a manner of speaking. And, well, much more, hence more trouble."

"Interesting," Zara replied, studying me.

I decided to expedite our conversation. "We need your help. We are trying to get to Zaradorba. I have the coordinates, but we need to get them uploaded to our ship's navigational unit. The Empire has outlawed travel there, and Dr. Goggins was unable to override the coding that is in place that prevents it from completing our trip mapping."

"So what do you think, Zara?" asked Goggins.

"I say your robot is very unique." She leaned toward me. "Aren't you?"

"Perhaps," I answered.

"Perhaps? Perhaps even rogue. I would love to help you and take a peek into your code."

Honora cleared her throat. "Well, he's not to be noodled with, Zara. And we are in a bit of a rush. If you are really good, I expect you to have this hack completed in an hour, two hours tops." She winked at me. "Again, what say you?"

Zara looked Honora up and down and smiled. "And who do we have here? Let me guess, coder girl, right? Top of your class but woefully misunderstood by all?"

Honora gulped. She was just pegged by Zara.

"My name is Honora. This is my brother, Alex. Don't mess with him. He likes guns. And this is my little sister, Talia. Don't mess with her, well, because I'll sic Alex on you if you do."

"Honora! Please, didn't your parents teach

you manners? We need Zara's help," Goggins exclaimed.

"We don't need her," Honora said as she crossed her arms.

"Stand down, Honora," I commanded. I turned to Zara. "Well?"

"Of course, I'll help you. I'm here, aren't I? And any enemy of the Empire is a friend of mine. And as far as you, coder-girl, I'm going to sit back and tell you what to do while you do the coding. How about that?"

Honora thought for a second and then said, "Fine."

Talia turned her arm comm to Zara. "I like your purple cape." Talia smiled as her new cici-chimp pet sat on her shoulder and nuzzled into her neck.

Zara calculated quickly that Talia was deaf, and her lips pursed together. I felt her bio-stats change. Her blood pressure dropped, and her heart quickened in pace. She had a maternal instinct that I was picking up on.

"Thank you, Talia. I love purple too." She turned to Goggins. "And if I'm able to successfully hack your ship's system, I would expect a little reward."

Goggins loosed his collar a bit. "Of course, Zara, of course. Um, how much are you thinking?"

"How much what?"

"Well, money, of course," he responded.

"I don't want money. I have plenty of money. More than I could ever spend."

"Dr. Goggins told us the Empire never did find the money you stole," quipped Alex.

Zara shot him a glance. "It wasn't their money. It was my parents' money, money that they stole from them. I decided to take back what they stole. Is that okay by you, soldier-boy?"

Alex squirmed in his chair. "Yeah, I guess."

She tipped his drink over.

Alex tried to catch it, but he was too slow. "Ah," he screamed. The drink spilled over his lap. Talia's cicichimp chirped in laughter.

Zara proved her point, even if it was in an adolescent way. "You're all wet, soldier-boy."

"Enough," I said strongly. "What do you want?"

Zara looked at Goggins for direction. "It's in charge, not me," Goggins confessed. "I just hopped along on his ship until things cool down in Heragi. Their parents, the Kells, created him. I coded just a part of him."

"It's no ordinary nanny-bot, is it?" she asked but knew the answer already.

"No, you surmised correctly earlier. It's rogue," Goggins said as he took the last swig of his drink.

Right then, Feti's voice came through on my internal comms system. "Gabe, a Heragi military ship has landed at the Emeraz Base planet-port."

"Thank you, Feti. We're on our way. Begin your lift off procedures," I said.

"Copy that," Feti replied.

"Time to go, everyone," said Goggins.

"Again, what do you want?" I leaned toward Zara.

Zara took a look around the street. "Let me think about it. Now lead me to your ship." She stood up and pulled her cape around her.

I took the lead and led them all out of the cafe. I scanned the street and began our trek to the ship.

"Shouldn't we walk a bit faster, or a better thought, shouldn't we run?" asked Goggins.

"No. We don't want to attract attention. Once we're outside the city, we will double-time it," I replied. I looked back to check on the children and that Alex had the back sweep position. He was doing a good job scanning the crowd without being suspicious as he guarded any activity behind us.

We again passed by the wealthy couple who were still conducting an afternoon stroll through the streets with townspeople bowing their heads. The street was busy and filled with a shift change of mining employees.

Goggins asked Zara a question that I also was about to query her on. "Who is that couple?"

I turned around and saw that Zara had draped her cape around her face with only her eyes showing.

She whispered, "They are the Farushabs. Leo and Nel. Just bow if they make eye contact with you."

"Why should we?" asked Honora.

"Because they own the planet," said Zara.

"Own the planet?" asked Goggins. "How is that possible?"

"It wasn't easy, but we were able to arrange it," she said.

"We? Did you help them?" Goggins hissed.

"Yes, I had to. They offered me sanctuary here. No extradition. At least as long as I keep their financial system humming along with no hiccups."

"So they're your friends," Goggins said with a smile.

"They are now. But they won't be shortly," said Zara.

We exited the town without causing notice. We walked in a normal fashion for a few minutes, then I shouted back to everyone, "Okay, we're clear. No time to waste now. Keep up with my pace." I looked back at Honora. "Do you have Talia's hand?"

"Yes," she shouted.

"Time to run," I yelled.

Feti had the ship door down in anticipation of our arrival. We ran up the ramp and all moved into the bridge of the ship.

Zara went into action and pulled out her coder. She looked up to me and said, "Well?"

I knew she wanted the Kells' navigation code to Zaradorba. I stuck out my arm, and she inserted a wire that connected to her drive to begin the download. I called up the navigational sequence to Zaradorba and allowed her to access the sequence.

"Got it," she said as she pulled her wire sharply from my arm.

Ouch. I thought that but didn't say it. She didn't know about my pain attributes yet. And I didn't want her to.

"Feti, this is Zara. She's going to be helping with your navigational program."

"Copy that, Gabe," it said. "Hello, Zara, nice to meet you."

"Nice to meet you too, Feti. Now this won't hurt a bit."

"I don't feel pain, unlike Gabe," it said.

"Is that so?" said Zara, turning to me. She smiled.

Well, the cat was out of the bag on that one.

Zara inserted her coding device into Feti's navigational board. She then turned to Honora and said, "Okay, hotshot, are you ready?"

Honora jumped up from her seat. "Yeah, I'm ready."

"Okay, let's go. Sit right down and take this coder," instructed Zara.

"I got my own," said Honora as she pulled out her own coding device. Zara was impressed.

Honora hopped into her seat and settled in. I reviewed her bio-metrics. Her nervous system was rising, but I could see she was fighting it, and it began to stabilize.

"Open Feti's overall directory," said Zara.

Honora coded furiously. I leaned back into the commander seat and surveyed Alex. He was looking out the window, watching for anyone or thing approaching. I looked over to Talia. She was playing with her cicichimp. I was glad she had something to keep her company.

I opened Talia's directory. It was sparser than the others. Perhaps, I thought, because she was younger. She had years more to have it grow. I reviewed her academic record. Above average grades. Her deafness was medically outlined in detail.

Deafness had been mostly eliminated across the Heragi Empire with advanced medical treatments. Mechanical devices worked to solve the issue ninety-nine percent of the time, but Talia's first operation was not successful at the age of two years. It had, in fact, gone terribly wrong and caused more damage. But there was no malice for the surgeon. The file noted an abnormality in Talia's blood type and DNA that caused the surgery not to take.

Damiel and Ava taught their child the universal sign language, but they also developed a unique sign language that only their family understood. And Ava put that sign language in my records as well. Of course, transceivers worked well for Talia when it came to school and functioning in society, as did her ability to read lips. Talia was often caught daydreaming in school and at times, she had grand mal seizures that they attribute to the damage done during the surgery when she was an infant.

I looked up to watch Talia play with her newfound pet. She looked over at me and smiled.

Back to Talia's folder director — there was a file called Talia Talk. It contained code. I would need to wait on that upload.

I tuned back in to the coding work that Zara and Honora were working on.

"No, never cross the d string code with that elemental code. That will trigger a lock out. Then you're screwed or we're screwed," Zara schooled Honora.

"Okay, got it," she said as her hands kept flying across her coder.

"Gabe, warning," Feti interrupted. "A military ship is approaching. On board, there are ten military-bots and two humans."

Alex jumped and peered out harder. "I see them," he shouted.

I moved to the window and saw their ship land. The military-bots ran out and took a stance to fire upon the ship.

"Everyone, buckle up. Time to move. Honora, the coding session is over. We'll have to continue later. Prepare for lift off."

"Wait, what about Zara?" Goggins asked. "We need to let her off the ship."

"No, I'm good," said Zara as she strapped herself in.

"What do you mean?" asked Goggins

"Well, that payment for the navigational hack? Getting off planet is the payment. I need to get dropped off at Suissey," she said.

"Suissey? Aren't you wanted there too?" asked Goggins.

"Suissey? No…they recruited me. They need hacker skills to stop the other hackers."

"But you stole from their bank!" said Goggins.

"That just showed them how good I was. They have insurance. It's all a shell game, Goggins, haven't you learned that yet?" She laughed.

"And what about that filthy rich couple — the

Farushabs?" he asked.

"Them? Well, they won't like that I'm leaving. And they won't like you all for helping me leave either. Sorry about that. But if you have the Empire after you, then adding the Farushabs to the list of your haters can't be all that bad, right?"

"No, not at all. We'll just add them to the list," said Goggins.

I looked out the window. Foxwell and Special Agent Jakawa marched down the ramp of their ship. Foxwell ordered his bots to open fire.

The bots fired as they approached the *Alyssia*. They were aiming for our engines.

Feti piped up, "Gabe, we should lift off now or the lasers could cause damage to our engines."

"I agree, Feti," I said, and we took off hard. Everyone jolted back into their seats.

Alex looked back to the ground. "They're boarding their ship," he shouted.

I pulled us out of the atmosphere and into space as fast as Feti's systems could allow.

"Where are we going?" cried Goggins.

"To Suissey," I replied.

Then we all heard the screech of the cicichimp. I looked over to Talia. She was holding onto it tight during liftoff.

"Well, what's one more anyway?" I said.

The cicichimp screeched some more before being comforted by Talia.

I set a course to Suissey. Foxwell's ship was soon behind us.

"Gabe, we've been hailed by the ship following us. They want to talk," Feti stated.

"What? Don't talk with them," hissed Goggins.

I turned to Alex. "What would they want, Alex?"

He scratched his head. "Well, to understand who they are dealing with. You, namely. Then they will want to find your weakness or a weakness in our plan or even with the ship. Last, they will try to negotiate."

"Thank you," I told him.

Alex sat a bit taller in his chair.

"Feti, are there combat abilities on this ship that are not part of the original design? Something that Edward Gates kept a secret from planet-port authorities?" I asked.

"Yes, this ship has full military-grade weapons, missiles, and evasive systems," Feti confessed.

"Put them online and prep them for use," I

instructed.

We heard one of the walls move, and a laser turret opened with a seat that popped up.

"Thank you, Feti. Is that turret automatic or manual?" I asked.

"Either configuration, Gabe."

"Thank you. Alex, can you operate that?"

Alex lit up. "Yes, sir. I mean, yes, Gabe." He unbuckled from his belt and jumped into the turret, hitting buttons and fingering controls as he got familiar with the system.

"Feti, connect us to the ship, audio only," I told it.

"Affirmative, connecting now," Feti replied.

"This is General Foxwell of the Heragi Navy and commander of the *Firestone*. And who am I connected with?"

I thought for a moment. How should I introduce myself? There were no scripts from Ava or Damiel in my files.

"This is GBE-11 Guard Bot E Series number 11. I'm commanding the *Alyssia*, for now. You may call me Gabe," I said. Perhaps the *for now* addition wasn't a good wording choice. Well, it was done. He knew my name and serial number.

"Is there a human I can talk to on the ship?"

he asked.

"I am the leader for our team," I responded.

There was a pause.

"Well, um, Gabe. You're causing a lot of trouble that seems to keep mounting. You stole a hovercraft down on Heragi. You stole the *Alyssia*, which I'm sure Mr. Gates isn't too happy about, and you have the Kell children, who are wanted by the Empire. Do you want me to go on?"

"No," I replied.

"Wait, and I believe you have illegal code in your system. Which means, Mr. Gabe, that you are rogue. And rogue robots are illegal in the Heragi Empire."

Another pause.

I turned and saw their ship was gaining on us. I looked at Alex and pointed to the *Firestone*. He nodded and prepared to open fire. His blood pressure rose. He was nervous. I checked everyone's bio-metric levels and, of course, they were all elevated. Nothing I could do about that but get us out of the situation.

Zara glanced at me. Her vitals were the calmest. She had the heart of a hacker who had been in hot water in the past. Goggins had sweat on his brow even though the bridge was kept cool for humans. Honora was coding fast and furious, continuing to crack the navigational system. Talia and the cicichimp were nestled into each other, and Talia's bio-levels were the lowest of all the children. I made a note of that to review later.

"I understand your concern, General," I replied.

"I was wondering, partner, if we could talk, in-person, so we could sort all this out. I'm sure the kids miss their parents and are wondering how they are doing, and I suspect vice-versa. What do you say?" negotiated Foxwell.

"The children are fine," I replied.

"Well, I will need some actual proof of that. Why don't you turn on your cameras so I can see them?"

"No, General."

"Well, um, Gabe, then you leave me no choice but to board your ship. Be prepared for our docking."

"That wouldn't be a good idea, General," I told him.

"And why would that be?"

"Because we're prepared to fight. Fair warning, Foxwell," I said.

I heard him laugh. He wanted to hear me

laugh. "Well, Gabe. Now, you may be an exceptional robot, but I have ten bots on this combat ship. And you have three children. Three special children who I'm sure you don't want harmed. That would go against your main directive, I'm guessing. Correct?" Foxwell shouted an order he also wanted me to hear. "Prepare to dock and board the *Alyssia*."

"Correct, Foxwell, but there may be something you don't know." I turned to Alex and yelled, "Now!"

Alex opened fire on the *Firestone*, spraying a pattern against their starboard engine.

Foxwell's audio was still on. "Ahh, shields up! Shields up! Dammit, system report, system report, pronto!"

Alex continued shooting.

Honora jumped out of her seat. "I did it, I did it. I cracked the navigational system!" Honora turned to Zara, who gave her a high five.

"Excellent work, kid."

"Thank goodness," said Goggins, wiping his sweat.

"Stop!" I shouted, putting one of my fingers to my mouth to silence them all. "Feti, turn off our comms link to the general."

"Affirmative, Gabe. Comms have been cut. The general's ship's engine is disabled."

Everyone cheered and Alex jumped out of his turret chair, enthused with his accomplishments. Alex, Honora, and Talia hugged.

I turned back to the console. "Feti, continue our course to Suissey. And then after that stop, onward to Zaradorba."

The cicichimp let out three small screeches. The children laughed.

Feti turned the ship toward planet Suissey.

I looked back at Foxwell's ship as it slid off our pathway and was stalled in space.

Alex sat next to me in the co-commander seat. He deserved to sit there.

"You're an enemy of the state now. I'm sorry we needed you to fight and fire on the general," I said to him.

"I'm not," he replied. "I must trust what my parents were preparing us for, what they were trying to save us from. Yes, I'm now an enemy like you. Rogue, but in a different way. In my mind and my heart."

I contemplated what he said. Yes, we were now both rogue. All of us on the ship were rogue.

6

———

The voyage to Suissey would take a sol day.

After a festive meal that Feti made for the humans and cicichimp, they found private cabins to rest in.

I stayed at the bridge. I monitored the navigation. Everything seemed to be working correctly. I decided to review more of Talia's files. I opened the directory and the Talia Talk code.

I reviewed the lines. It was code to upload into my system and not her transceiver, which surprised me. Also in the file were a video and audio file that I had not seen earlier. The file was called *play this first*. So I played it.

Ava appeared on my vision.

Ah, Ava. I felt my nervous system levels proceed into an almost meditative rhythm. She had that effect on me. But also, a small pain developed in my chest. Ouch. I wished I would get warned before I felt pain. Nonetheless, it was worth it if I got to see Ava.

She smiled. If I could smile, I would smile back. She began, "Gabe. If you are hearing this, then your mission has been activated. And you will have seen the code in this file. This code is for you alone. Trigger the upload after listening to the information I'm about to share."

I paused the video and scanned the bridge and adjoining hallway for human bio-metrics. Everyone must be asleep.

I resumed the video. Ava spoke again. "As you have observed, Talia is deaf. You must have read her surgery history and her medical records. But there is something else we wanted to tell you."

At that moment, Damiel stepped into the video and sat down next to Ava. "Hello, Gabe," he said to the camera.

"Damiel is going to explain some, well, enhancements that Talia has." She hesitated. "Damiel, go ahead."

"Yes, I developed a sensor, and I inserted it into Talia's brain next to the chip she already has to communicate with her arm comm. It won't harm her. It's undetectable, at least with current technology on Heragi. And this sensor is activated by the code that is in this file. This code will allow you to communicate directly with Talia. Essentially, it's a speech comm device just for you and Talia."

Ava interrupted him. "It goes beyond that, really. It will be her thoughts before she has formulated speech."

"Yes," said Damiel. "That is correct. It's a telepathic connection, really. First of its kind, at least on Heragi. Other alien species have this naturally. We on Heragi used to have this ability. Some say other humanoids in our galaxy have it as well. But here on Heragi, over the past century, we have had our DNA strands bio-engineered, so we have lost these ancient abilities. That is one of the reasons we sent you on this mission."

Ava said, "When Talia had surgery, it was apparent her DNA was different. She has the telepathic DNA strands, but she needs the code to reboot her abilities. Eventually, she won't need the sensor, and her DNA will take over naturally. She will be telepathic with anyone who can receive it. You will be the first one she can communicate with — to practice with, really. There is a telepathic range, we believe, which is within eyesight of each other, but there is so much we don't know. It's all new to us as well."

"As you know, being telepathic is forbidden in the Heragi Empire," said Damiel.

"We want to give Talia back her galaxy-given abilities. So maybe it will give her a fighting chance against the Empire or an advantage, if she ever needs it," said Ava.

I paused the video again. I needed to absorb this information. If or *when* I uploaded this code, then Talia would become an enemy of the state along with her brother and sister. She would have rogue code activated in her. I sighed.

It was part of the mission. It must be. But somehow, I felt I was sentencing her. And I was sure that was how her parents felt, too. I resumed the video.

Ava continued, "We wanted you to be prepared before you loaded the code. You will have a special bond. You will need this to complete your mission. That is why we built the sensor that is placed in Talia. Many years ago, we monitored

Talia, and she was communicating or meditating with animals and trees. You may notice she has a special ability for this. When we conducted further testing on her, we found that her abilities didn't have to stop with just animals and nature. Her DNA had an additional strand. We don't know why but from either my DNA or Damiel's, it is there."

I caught the sounds of small steps coming down the hallway. I stopped the video. The cicichimp jumped on my lap, causing me to flinch. I had never held an animal. It cuddled up to my chest. Curious, I thought.

Talia was coming. I sensed her bio-metrics. She also curled up in my lap. She put her arms around the cicichimp. Ava must have programmed an instinctive program of comfort into my system. My arms curled around them both and my armor began to heat up to keep them warm.

I continued the video.

Ava's speech resumed. "Take care of her. She will need you as she becomes aware of her power." Ava forced a smile. Perhaps to give me hope. The video ended with Damiel putting his arm around his wife.

"Thank you, Gabe," he said. The video stopped.

I looked down on Talia and the cicichimp and then upward out to space. I activated the code, and the upload began.

I felt my CPU speed up as the coding started. I never felt this disorientated before, and I had had plenty of coding work done by the Kells and even Dr. Goggins. Code uplifted into multiple systems, and I felt six new areas get inserted throughout my body. My system went back to normal after what I calculated was ten minutes. I must have panicked a bit because I slightly bumped the cicichimp and Talia as I jolted awake.

To say I felt different was an understatement. I touched my hand to my head. My brain felt like it had been rewired. I looked down to my lap.

Talia was looking straight at me.

Her eyes rolled back into her head. At first, I thought she was having a seizure, but then I remembered the Kells said uploading my new code would activate the sensor in her spinal cord. I held her shoulders up to look at her face to face.

Her face became calm, and her eyes rolled back correctly into place. She opened her eyes and locked onto mine.

Ow, she said or rather, she thought.

Are you okay? I sensed back to her.

Her eyes bugged open. *Ahh.* I felt her shout.

It's okay, don't be frightened. Your parents have put a sensor in your body so that we can communicate. It's okay, I thought to her.

What?

I'm guessing this is similar to how you communicate with animals, like cicichimps, correct? I thought to her.

Yes, she thought back. *So you can hear me?*

Yes, in a sense. I feel your thoughts and then they formulate in my brain as words.

It's true that I've always been able to talk with animals and the trees, rocks and wind. But never to anyone else. Never to Mom or Dad. Can I talk with them?

Maybe in the future. But right now, it's only me.

She petted the cicichimp. *Can you communicate with a cicichimp?* she asked.

I hadn't thought of that. I was curious too. I might as well try. I looked down at the cicichimp, who stared up to me.

Hello, I thought. *My name is Gabe.*

It looked at Talia, who nodded in encouragement. Then I heard its thoughts. *I've never talked with a robot before. You are so big! Nice to meet you.*

Talia *laughed,* silently on the bridge but loudly in my brain. We all laughed together.

Talia, I thought, *your parents know that you are special.*

I'm deaf, said Talia.

You're not just deaf. Your telepathic gift is very special and rare. You know that, right?

Yes. I tried to tell one of my school teachers but she thought I had an error in my transceiver. I told my parents and they told me just to keep it a secret and not even to tell Honora or Alex. Can I tell them now?

Your parents didn't say not to tell them. Although I'm hesitant to tell Dr. Goggins and Zara. Let's wait and keep it between us for now, I explained.

Okay. But one day, will I be able to talk with them too?

I don't know. I hope so, Talia, I answered truthfully.

I heard and felt stirring on the ship. Everyone was waking up.

Talia took the cicichimp into her arms and

scooted down the hallway to greet everyone in the galley.

"Feti, cook them a nice breakfast, will you?" I asked.

"Yes, of course, Gabe. Mr. Gates has some very expensive and rare delicacies that I believe they will enjoy," it replied.

"Thank you, Feti."

"Gabe, I wanted you to be aware that there was some additional coding that took place on my systems over the past few hours."

"There was? What kind of coding?"

"On my comms system. I wasn't aware of it until I completed delta scan on a daily rotation that Mr. Gates had coded in me. It identifies any code changes over different intervals. It's undetectable and hidden in my system."

"What was the change, specifically?"

"A beacon has been put in place."

"Did you trigger it?"

"No, but I let the coder believe it was initiated. I planned on telling you as soon as possible."

"Who was the coder?" I asked.

"I don't know. That's the problem. They put in circuitous identification. I can't trace who or what area of the ship the coder was in. Only that it was done."

Who would do this? Zara didn't want to be caught with us. Unless she believed there was a bounty from the general, but that may put her more at risk with the Farushabs. Honora wouldn't want to be caught. Goggins, he may want both a bounty and to make a deal with Foxwell. It had to be him.

"Thank you, Feti. Let's keep this between us."

"Affirmative, Gabe."

"Alert me when we start our approach to Suissey."

"Yes, I will."

I got up and headed down the hallway toward the galley. I heard discussions and laughter from the humans and chirps from the cicichimp.

I entered the galley and took a seat at the table. Indeed, everyone was enjoying the breakfast Feti had served up to them in the food conveyer.

"I regret that you don't eat, Gabe. This is absolutely fantastic," said Goggins as he spooned a mouthful of food into his face.

"Cece likes the fruit juice cocktail," Talia played from her arm comm.

"Good morning, Gabe," said Goggins with a

smile. "Isn't it strange to say good morning in space?"

"Yeah, maybe we should say *Good Space,* instead," said Honora.

"Or *top of the space to you,*" chatted back Goggins. Everyone groaned at his suggestion.

"How did you sleep, Dr. Goggins?" I asked.

"Well, I got a bit of a crick in my neck because Mr. Gates apparently doesn't believe in more than one pillow per bed. Perhaps you could work it out for me, Gabe. I could code a masseuse program in you. That would be helpful. What do you say?"

"No, I may hurt you," I responded.

"Well, I would code it so you wouldn't hurt me," Goggins responded.

"Are we nearing Suissey?" asked Alex.

"We should be arriving shortly. Feti will notify me when we get within range," I replied.

A thought from Talia came through to me. *You believe Dr. Goggins did something…re-coded Feti?*

I turned to her and almost spoke out loud. Her voice seemed to come so clearly to me that I forgot our minds were now linked. I sent a thought her way. *I'm not exactly sure. Someone coded Feti to send out a comm ping for us to be tracked. If Foxwell's ship comes within range of ours, then they could pick up on it. I had Feti disable it.*

You believe Goggins did it?

Yes.

Are you going to ask him?

Now?

Yes, now.

I was going to wait.

For what? If he's guilty, we can leave him on Suissey. If he didn't do it, then you will have more time to figure this out.

She was right. I looked at her and nodded. She was far more mature than I had first thought. I wondered if she just heard that thought. I glanced at her and she smiled. She had. Hmmm, I wondered if I could ever shield my thoughts from her. Darn, she probably heard that too.

Yes, I did, she replied.

"Dr. Goggins, did you happen to do any coding last night?" I asked. Everyone stopped eating.

Goggins put down his drink and spilled part of it on his sleeve. "Frazzle! Sorry kids. My language. Gabe, no I wasn't doing any coding. Why do you ask? Is there something wrong?"

"Yes, there is. Feti reported to me that someone had been re-coding the comm system earlier and sent out a ping that gives our coordinates to be picked up by a nearby ship. And I would like to know who did it and why."

Everyone was silent. The children's eyes darted between Goggins and Zara.

"It can't be Honora," stated Alex. I observed his protectiveness levels rise for his sister.

"Of course, it wasn't me. Why would I want that Foxwell fellow to find us?" she defended herself.

"Feti can't tell you who did the coding?" asked Zara as she continued eating.

"No, it couldn't decipher that. It was a clean hack. No trace. Someone knew what they were doing and had the skill to pull it off," I explained.

"It wasn't me, Gabe, I swear. I mean, why would I want that?" Goggins spouted out.

"To cut a deal, negotiate. To sell us out and save your hide," Alex said as he got up and leaned against the galley window.

"No, no. I wouldn't do that. Now that I've gotten to know you all a bit, I wouldn't do that," pleaded Goggins. "And really, I'm not that good of a coder."

"He's right about that," defended Zara. "He's good but not that good. Feti's code is pretty locked up," she added.

"I can testify to that. Feti's code is tight. I don't think he could have done it either," said Honora.

"Thank you, Honora. I never thought I would be grateful to hear criticism," said Goggins, running his hands through his hair.

"I'm not a fan, Dr. Goggins. Just telling the facts," Honora said as she stared him down.

Goggins swallowed. "Um, sure. I can respect that." He bowed his head in deference to the teenager.

Who could it be? I thought.

Talia thought back, *Maybe it's no one on board*.

True, that is a possibility, I replied.

"We'll table this discussion. Let's prepare for landing. We're coming upon Suissey shortly. We'll drop off Zara and begin our trip to Zaradorba," I said.

Goggins and the children left the galley.

Zara lingered as she looked out the window at

planet Suissey getting closer. She turned to me. "I want to thank you for bringing me here," she said.

"Thank you for your assistance," I replied.

"There is one more thing I could use your help with."

"I need to get the children to their uncle as soon as possible," I replied. "We've already been delayed longer than expected."

"It may be of assistance to you too," she replied, getting closer.

"What is it?" I asked.

"There is someone on Suissey who needs my, I mean our, help. She's being held captive." She turned down her head and looked out to the approaching planet.

"Who is it?" I asked.

"Her name is Synthia. She raised me after my parents died. She's a telepath."

7
———

"Who took her and why?" I asked Zara.

I needed more information about why we should risk the mission to rescue her friend, even if Zara believed somehow it could also assist us.

"The Suissey government took her two months ago. They kidnapped her from Plexethium. I believe they are exploiting her telepathic skills. The Heragi Empire made an alliance with the Suissey planet," she explained.

I checked her bio-metrics. There was no rise in her nervous system or temperature. From reviewing those metrics, it appeared she wasn't lying unless she was very good at controlling her brain waves and body system, which could be a possibility if she was trained properly.

"And why should I risk my mission to rescue her?" I replied as I exited the galley and turned down the hallway to the bridge.

Zara followed behind me and then ran in front of me and stopped me cold. "She has special skills that could help you," she said with her feet firmly planted. Zara had some military fighting training. I could tell with her balanced stance. "Specifically, Synthia's skills could help Talia."

I gently swept her to the side of the hallway so she wouldn't see it as an attack. I kept walking. "Excuse me. And how is that?"

"I know what is going on between you and Talia," she said.

"What?"

"You heard me, robot," she replied. "Your little secret game of telepathy."

I stopped and turned around to face her.

"I picked up on it in your code when you gave me your navigational coordinates to Zaradorba. I also detected a sensor in Talia's brain stem when I ran bio-metrics on the children. Is your code somehow connected to that sensor?" she asked.

I leaned in to her.

"Sorry, I always like to know who I travel with. It's a bit nosy but I find it informs me," she said as she took a step back and raised her hands into fists, probably not knowing if I would send a blow her way or not.

I would not. At least not now.

Zara surprised me. That was probably why she angered me. She was smart, but I had no idea she would have bio-scanning equipment in her coder. And that she would use it on the children. I was also naive to think she wouldn't try to access my code. Hackers hack. That's what they do. Her curiosity may be her undoing one day with the wrong person — or robot.

I had to admit she was most intriguing. I could understand why Dr. Goggins was attracted to her. But I needed to watch her more closely.

"You're correct," I said. "She has enhanced abilities with the aid of the sensor. And with my coding, we can communicate telepathically. And how could Synthia help Talia?"

"She could help her develop her telepathic skills so she wouldn't need her sensor. You could then remove it surgically, and she would be undetectable to bio scans. Synthia would help her perfect her telepathy and more. Then she would become powerful. More powerful than any Heragi human has been in decades. That could help her find and rescue her parents and those the Heragi have oppressed." She dropped her hands.

"My mission is not to save her parents or the Heragi people — if they even want to be saved. But if it will help Talia, then I would be in favor of rescuing your friend. Can you promise Synthia would train her?"

"I can't promise, but we can plead our case to her," she said.

I paused. Talia was the most vulnerable of all the children. And the Kells were most worried about her and the possibility that if she would be captured by the Heragi Empire, they would use her potential skills for their galaxy dominance.

I reviewed the pros and cons quickly. There was risk. And there was a tactical benefit if we succeeded as well.

"Let us ask the children. Talia will be the ultimate decision maker." I turned and headed toward the bridge.

Feti had started the landing protocols before I reached my commander seat.

I strapped into my seat. Zara slid into her chair and buckled up as well.

"Feti, take us in to their planet-port. Zara, we need to scramble the *Alyssia*'s identification number. Can you give us an alternate one that can't be traced to Heragi?"

"I can," yelled Honora.

"Go for it," said Zara.

I looked around and nodded to Honora. "You may proceed. No disrespect, but I want Zara to check your code," I explained.

Honora was already pounding out the code. Zara pointed at her. "Look at that one go." She leaned over, reviewed Honora's code, and pointed out a few items for her to fix.

"Gabe," said Feti. "We have the Suissey planet-port in the city of Jankai asking for our ship's identification number and flight plans. They want them immediately or they will fire upon us," it stressed.

"That seems a little harsh, doesn't it?" asked Goggins.

"Smart move, tactically," said Alex.

Talia hugged the cicichimp tight. Her bio levels were rising. I sent a thought to her. *It will be okay, Talia.*

She sent back a thought instantly. *I hope so.*

"Honora, we need that code now." I raised my voice level to overcome our landing throttle.

Honora kept pounding on her keyboard. "Got it!" she yelled.

"Looks good," seconded Zara.

"Uploading." Honora connected her code with Feti's system.

"Thank you, Honora. Uploading to Suissey planet-port officials," said Feti.

There was a five second pause that passed like an hour.

"Accepted," Feti replied.

Everyone sighed, including me.

"Land the *Alyssia*," I told Feti.

"Affirmative, Gabe," it replied.

Feti landed the *Alyssia*, and I gave instructions to Feti. "Same protocols as before. Notify me if there are any Heragi ships landing on Suissey or anything out of the ordinary."

"Affirmative, Gabe," replied Feti.

The children, Goggins, and Zara unbuckled their shoulder straps and stood.

"So, I guess this is goodbye, Zara. Until we meet again," said Goggins as he stuck out his hand to shake hers.

Zara took his hand in both of hers. "Our good-byes may have to wait a bit," she explained.

"What gives?" Alex asked.

"There's someone we need to pick up here —" I started to explain before being interrupted by Honora.

"We need to get to Zaradorba to see Uncle Jeb. We need to rescue Mom and Dad as soon as possible," she pointed out with a strain in her voice.

Alex took two steps toward me. "Who is it? And are they really a priority?"

Zara spoke up. "It's my friend. She's being held captive by the Suissey government. She could aid you in your mission. To reach your uncle."

"And how is that?" asked Goggins.

Talia was searching my mind. I felt her in it. She searched my thoughts. I would have liked to keep my thoughts private but giving Talia a heads up on the topic at hand may be best. *Talia, I have a question for you.*

She looked at me with surprise.

I turned to her. "Zara's friend can help Talia," I said out loud.

"What? Why does Talia need help?" asked

Honora, who put her hand on her sister's shoulder.

"Is something wrong?" asked Alex. "Tell us if there is."

"No, nothing is wrong with Talia," I said.

"My friend's name is Synthia. She's telepathic," started Zara.

"You mentioned that before. So?" said Honora.

I reviewed Talia's bio-metrics, and they were rising along with her siblings' metrics. I searched Talia's mind for her thoughts. She was open. No judgment. I only felt that she was curious, then a question came from her. *Who is this woman?*

"Zara believes that Suissey is collaborating with the Heragi Empire, and they're using Synthia's telepathy skills against her will," I said.

Zara cut me off. "She's a good person. She taught me many things. I don't have the telepathic gift, but for those who do, she's a teacher." She looked at Talia, who was stroking the cicichimp.

"Talia is telepathic?" asked Goggins.

"Not fully, yet, but she has the DNA strands," I said.

"She could be, with the right training. Having

this skill could help your parents and your uncle," explained Zara.

"And make her an enemy of the Empire," said Alex.

Honora kneeled down so Talia could read her lips. "Talia, I didn't know. None of us did."

Talia signed, *Mother and Father kept it a secret. But I kept secrets too.*

What secrets? Honora signed.

I can talk with animals, with trees and flowers, lots of things. It's always been that way.

Why didn't you tell us? signed Honora.

I thought I was crazy. I was afraid I would be sent off to the hospital again. And I didn't want to have any more operations.

Honora hugged her sister. *No more hospitals. Alex and I and Gabe will make sure of that.*

Alex spoke up. "Talia, do you want us to delay going to Zaradorba to rescue Synthia?"

Talia looked at everyone one by one. She nodded and signed, *Affirmative.*

"Then that settles it. Zara, where is Synthia being held?" I asked.

"She's in their financial headquarters. It holds all their digital intelligence and banking networks."

"How exactly is she helping the Suissey government? Surely being telepathic can't help with all the monetary transactions that happen in the trillions every day. Is she predicting the currency markets?" asked Goggins.

"They force her to read the minds of their enemies. Real or perceived enemies," she explained.

"She rats out people? Why does she give them up? She could refuse them," said Alex.

"They must have her drugged. I don't know," said Zara.

"How do you know all this?" asked Goggins.

Zara shot him a look.

"You hacked into their system," stated Honora.

"Yes," said Zara.

"But you told us you're going to go to work for them," stated Goggins, scratching his head.

"Yes, to gain access only. To free Synthia and to put an end to their practices. But having six people help spring Synthia is better than one, tactically speaking, right Alex?" asked Zara as she turned to him.

"Yes, that's true. But it will only benefit us if what she can offer is worth the risk," he evaluated.

Talia lifted her arm comm "No one will know. Until we find her. We must help Synthia."

"It's settled. We'll rescue Synthia," I said.

We exited the *Alyssia* and entered the city of Jankai.

"This way," Zara said as she took the lead. I kept close behind Zara with Goggins behind me, followed by the children with Alex as our rear guard.

I reviewed the statistics of the city of Jankai. Thirty million residents with daily financial travelers numbered in the tens of thousands. It was the financial district of the galaxy.

The city was shiny, clean, and cold. Not physically cold, but sterile cold. The infrastructure was the most advanced in all the galaxy because of its incredible wealth. Conveyor belts moved humans, bots, and alien species of every type to multiple city levels.

There was little petty crime since there was sophisticated surveillance by its homeland security department and the private security firms hired by the ultra-wealthy. I read an article saying there were a few high-stakes financial scams and identification thefts recorded recently, but there had not been a successful bank robbery in over three hundred years.

Every inch of surface in the city was monitored by video, audio, and bio-metrics. I felt my system scanned multiple times by corner bot units.

We hopped on a public transport bus and headed toward Suissey financial headquarters. I scanned the crowd on the bus. Many were work commuters or short-term business visitors. Suissey was not a relaxation destination. But because of the wealth of the business travelers, there was every luxury item available, from food to entertainment. All hours, all the time.

Honora sniffed the air as we got off the transport. "What is that smell?"

Goggins sniffed four times as he turned himself around. "That's oxylberries. Mmmm, delicious smell."

"Why would it smell like oxylberries here? I don't see anything resembling a tree, grass or bushes?" Honora said, looking around.

Zara explained, "They have aerial-bots that fly all around the city. They spray every district with a different smell. They believe it calms people's nervous systems."

"Why would they want to do that?" asked Alex.

"Money makes people nervous. Five hundred trillion credits are moved daily here. Losing money, making money, transferring money. You name it. These people look relaxed but inside, they are tight. Tight as a knot," she spit out.

We arrived at a looming black onyx building. Five hundred and fifty stories high.

"Blazes," said Alex as he looked up. "I can't see the top."

"That's okay. We're going down," Zara said.

"How far?" I inquired.

"Twenty-five floors," she said.

"That's pretty far down," Goggins said as he began to hyperventilate. He started taking deep breaths to calm himself down.

I stepped in front of our team. "Honora, you stay on the corner with Dr. Goggins and Talia. Alex, Zara and I are going in," I said. "Keep your comm device on. And if I tell you to retreat to the *Alyssia*, you follow my order, understand?"

"We won't leave you," Honora replied.

I stepped directly in front of her and leaned over until I was face to face with her.

"No, when I say retreat, you must follow that direction. Think of it as coming from your parents. They programmed me. They installed this mission into my brain, body and system. Do you understand?"

She pulled back, a bit afraid of my forcefulness. "Yes, Gabe. I understand," she said softly.

I put my hand on her shoulder and patted it. "I wouldn't leave you alone unless I knew I could trust you, okay?"

She nodded. "Yes."

"Honora's not in charge of me," stated Goggins with a huff. "I'm the adult here."

I turned swiftly and went eye to eye with Goggins. "You weren't invited on this mission, Dr. Goggins. You inserted yourself into it. You are not in charge of anything. Do you understand me?"

Goggins stumbled back and nearly fell over. "Um, yes, certainly, Gabe. We're all on the same team. I'll watch over Honora and Talia as if they were my own." He tried to smile.

A pair of police-bots were patrolling and stopped. They scanned me. I stood still.

I saw Alex put his hand down next to a hidden

gun. Zara reached behind her cape where I would have guessed she was hiding some kind of weapon.

The police-bots pinged my file sharing program. I pinged back a fake identification number. They reviewed my number and scanned it against any warrants. One of the bots looked at me and said, "Welcome to Jankai. Enjoy your stay."

"Thank you, we will," I replied. They walked away. "Okay, let's go."

We approached the entrance to the building, I turned my head to locate Honora, Goggins and Talia holding the cicichimp. I saw them on a corner, taking a seat at an outdoor café. At that moment, I caught Talia looking at me. She sent me a thought. *Good luck.*

I sent her back my thought. *Thank you. Get back to the ship safely if there are any problems.*

And with that last thought, I entered the building.

There were no security screenings, those were built into the walls, ceiling and floors, Zara explained to us. It was built this way to reduce any tension with the business travelers. They certainly spent a lot of money worrying about visitors and having zero trust in them.

"Don't we need security to get down to the twenty-fifth floor?" I asked.

"Yes, but I'm guessing my security clearance is already in the system since I start work here in two days," Zara commented. "Stay here."

Zara approached an information desk. A service-bot stood up to greet her. "How may I help you?" it asked.

"My name is Zara Lorgia. I just started working here, but I don't have my badge yet. Can you set me up with a temp badge?"

The service-bot typed her name into the building's security system. "It says here that you don't start for two days. You will receive it then," it flatly stated and sat down.

Zara turned around and furiously typed on her comm device. She hit the enter button hard and turned back to the service-bot. "But I'd really like to start today. No harm in getting a jump on my projects. As you can see from my profile, I work for Dr. Stefano. Do you know who that is?"

The bot didn't respond right away, then he said, "He's the director of the Suissey security department."

"Yes, correct. And I believe if you look a bit harder, you will find a note stating that I have his permission and clearance to start work today. Just to get a jump on the competition. Do you see it?"

The service-bot reviewed her file again. "I apologize. I did not see that note earlier. Yes, everything seems to be in order. Please place your eye next to this screen for verification."

"What? All these built-in bio-scans you have in the building don't already identify me?"

"No, those are just for monitoring current bio-metric levels," it replied.

"I'll have to put that at the top of my list to change," said Zara with a short grunt.

The service-bot replied, "Yes, Ms. Lorgia, that would be a fine improvement and would give me less to do."

"Well, I don't want to put you out of a job just yet," she said.

"No, of course not. Only when it is appropriate." It handed her the badge.

"One more thing. I have my nephew and his nanny-bot with me today. Can you give me two visitor badges?"

"I'm afraid not, Ms. Lorgia. They are not cleared for your floor in the basement. But they can go up to the visitor observation deck at the top."

"Yes, give me two badges for the deck. Thank you."

It handed her two badges "Here you are. And here is a map to follow to get you to the right elevators. Have a nice day."

"You have a nice day, too," Zara said as she waved at us and pointed for us to meet at a distant elevator.

"Did you secure three badges?" Alex asked.

"Not exactly. I have my badge that can take me below ground. But I could only get you two observation deck badges for the top of the building."

"Well, that is going in the wrong direction, isn't it?" said Alex as he pounded his hand against his leg.

"Hey, calm down, soldier-boy. Give me a second." She pulled her coder out from her cape. She looked at our badges and grabbed the numbers on them and pounded out some code. She hit the enter button on her coder which lit up the badges' digital chips.

"There. Give it a minute."

An elevator reached our main floor and opened. A few workers came out. A person had to badge individually to get on the elevator.

"Will this work?" asked Alex.

"We're about to find out," said Zara.

"Great," Alex replied.

Zara swiped her badge, and the elevator dinged a pleasant note, and a green light appeared. A female digital voice said, "Enter." Zara moved onto the elevator.

Alex swiped his pass over the scanner. The bell rang, and the female voice told him to enter the elevator.

My turn. I swiped, and a loud bell sounded off.

Three nearby security-bots looked my way.

Zara pulled her coder out and swiftly coded and hit the enter button.

"Swipe again," Zara whispered to me.

I swiped quickly, and the pleasant ding rang. The female bot invited me into the elevator.

I waved my arm to the three security-bots that were only ten yards away from me. Zara popped her head out of the elevator and yelled to the security-bots, "It's fine. Just a glitch! Technology, huh? Get that fixed, will ya?"

The security-bots stopped, and the elevator door closed.

Zara hit the twenty-fifth underground floor button.

The elevator bell rang.
The door opened.
We drew our weapons.

8

I was the first to step forward on the underground twenty-fifth floor of the Suissey financial head-quarters building.

I scanned the elevator hallway, and it was empty. I motioned for Zara and Alex to follow. We proceeded from the hallway into an open space that looked out upon the whole floor. There were bots, humans and aliens walking back and forth in front of huge consoles that showed the flow of currencies across the galaxy. Glass walls and doors revealed more computer consoles and screens in a long row of offices.

"Where is she?" asked Alex.

"Toward the end of this floor, there's a lab.

They call it the interview room. I think she's in there," Zara replied.

"Great," said Alex as he spun around to her. "So we are just going to go walking onto the floor like tourists?"

"Great idea," replied Zara as she took off walking.

"Gabe?" he implored me.

"Let's go," I said. "Conceal your weapons."

We hid our weapons and followed Zara. She strode forward like she belonged there. Technically, I guess she did — she was just two days early.

Some people glanced our way but didn't stop us as we crossed the large open floor. We reached the end of the room that had two steel double doors protected by security-bots.

Zara turned to us slightly. "Follow my lead."

"Do we have a choice?" snapped Alex.

I was taking bio-scans and recording how many bots, humans and aliens there were on the floor and each office that I could see into. So far, there were one hundred and twenty-one entities. Divided by three, that would be a lot for each of us to take down or wound.

"Take the sweep," I instructed Alex, and he

ducked behind me and scanned the room, probably trying to take in the same data I was calculating.

We approached the security-bots. They each held up an arm as we did.

"Authorized personnel only," said one of the security-bots.

"Here you go." Zara offered her employee badge.

The bot scanned it and nodded. "Zara Lorgia, you may enter."

"This is my assistant and lab-bot. They need entry as well," she stated passing by the bots.

They both stuck out their arms, preventing me and Alex from entering. "Stop," said one of them. The bots scanned our visitor badges.

"They do not have employee badges. These are visitor badges," stated the lead bot.

"Check again. I'm sure it's a mistake," she countered.

The lead bot, probably with a more advanced comm and reasoning CPU than its colleague bot, took two seconds to review her response and his stored responses.

"One moment, as I check our system," said the bot.

Zara shrugged slightly to me and Alex. "Go ahead," she said to the bot.

The bot pushed a few buttons on its forearm and talked into the embedded comm device. "Security check for the sub twenty-fifth."

"Checking, sub twenty-fifth," returned another bot voice.

Our bot scanned the badges again.

While we waited, I calculated what our escape plan was if this went sideways. I could take the two security-bots down and enter the room to find Synthia with Zara and Alex but how to get across this immense floor and back to the elevators, then up the elevator and out the ground floor did not calculate any successful outcomes.

"Zara Lorgia and the lab-bot have clearance for the interview room," stated the security-bot. "But clearance for the other human is not documented."

I turned to Alex and saw him tense up. He looked up to me with a furrowed brow. I sensed his bio-metrics rising higher.

Zara shrugged. "Mistakes happen. I'll get that fixed for tomorrow."

The bots let me pass. I turned to Alex. "We'll be right out. Stay here."

"Where the blazes would I be going?" he snorted back. He shook his head. "Sorry. Affirmative." He took a deep breath and retreated against the wall a few steps away from the security-bots and reviewed the room for any notable changes.

Zara and I entered the interview room.

It was a large room that had five other glass enclosed rooms within it. Medical equipment and chairs outfitted with restraining belts for arms and legs. Interesting interview room, I thought, not that I had anything to compare it against.

We headed down the center pathway. Various aliens and humans were strapped into the chairs, some in comatose states or close to it. Employees huddled around certain captives while others scurried around watching the bio-monitors on the wall that were connected to their interviewees.

A man in a white lab coat approached us. "May I help you?" he asked Zara.

"My name is Zara Lorgia. I'm the new galaxy transaction analyst. This is my assistant," she told the man.

"Yes, Zara. I didn't recognize you since our interview. Apologies for the meek job title for the actual role you will be filling here." He snorted.

"Yes, well, I think the government wants to

keep what I actually do as quiet as possible. What's a title anyway, right?" She laughed.

"Well, welcome," he said.

"Nice to be here, Dr. Stefano," she said.

"And who do we have here?" Stefano looked at me.

"My coding assistant. I never leave home without him," she said with a smile as she patted me on the shoulder.

"Okay. Fine." He dismissed my presence quickly. "I'll take you to your desk." He marched us back to a corner desk with multiple monitors. "And what exactly will you be doing for us, again?"

"Merging you with the Heragi financial system," she said.

"You mean us, correct?"

"Right, merging us with the Heragi financial system and going into the backend of other planetary financial systems. Making sure the populations' bio-metrics are attached to their accounts," she said.

"Yes, you're the hacker extraordinaire." He looked her over closely.

"My coding will blow you away," she said with a smile.

He belly laughed. "I look forward to inspecting your work closely. And also, I have a pet project I would like your help on. I'd like to somehow connect these interviewees' brains to our security system. There has to be lots of additional information we could retrieve in a more efficient manner than our rudimentary ways."

"Yeah, sure, sounds good," said Zara.

"Great. Well, good luck. Ignore what you see here. It will help you sleep better," he said with a grin as he pointed to the interview chairs. "Maybe we can have dinner together sometime soon."

"Yeah, after I unpack and get settled in," she said.

Stefano strolled away.

"Creep," Zara said under her breath.

Zara turned to her computer console to begin accessing the Suissey financial system.

I bio-scanned the floor. Many of the interviewees were close to death.

"Where is Synthia?" I asked.

Zara's fingers flew across her keyboard. "Trying to locate her now. Also throwing in some viruses that will take down this galactic embarrassment of a government."

A door at the end of the hallway opened slowly.

Stefano pushed an elderly woman in a wheelchair down the hallway toward the interviewees. Zara stopped coding. Her mouth dropped open. "That's her. Synthia. My God, she's aged," she whispered.

Synthia's eyes looked fogged and darted from side to side. Her gray hair was wrapped up in a hive bun. She wore a flowing dress that hid her legs. She locked eyes with Zara and then cast her eyes downward with no facial or bio-rhythm change that I could detect.

"I don't think she recognized you," I said. "Her bio-levels did not change at all when she looked at you."

Zara nodded.

Stefano wheeled Synthia up to a nearby interviewee, an alien who was squirming in the chair. I picked up on his language and found it in my language translator. He was a Beelayzian from a nearby planet. They weren't a warrior race but successful traders across the galaxy. His scaled body was off-color. He was dying.

Stefano gave Synthia direction. "You know what to do. Begin."

Synthia looked at the interviewee and cast her head downward.

Stefano hit the wheelchair. "I said begin."

Synthia lifted her right arm toward the Beelayzian. He looked over, terrorized. "Please, no, don't," he pleaded.

Synthia let her hand fall to her lap, "No, no more," she whispered.

"What did you say?" Stefano whipped her wheelchair around to face him.

She repeated it loud enough for the whole room to hear. "I said no. Enough."

"I will say when enough is enough," Stefano spit out. He grabbed an injection device and started for her arm. He jabbed it in. Synthia grimaced. He twirled her around to face the interviewee again.

A lab assistant asked the Beelayzian a question. "Did you deliver our investment codes to Zaradorba? Please answer yes or no."

"No," said the alien as he closed his eyes.

Synthia raised her right hand again up to the alien. The alien tried to pull away, but he was strapped into his chair tight.

Synthia flinched then brought her hand down.

"Well?" snapped Stefano.

She was silent. She closed her eyes.

He kicked her chair.

"He is lying. He gave it to a man named Fuollu who is back on Heragi," she whispered. She put her face into her hands and wept.

"No, that is not true," cried the Beelayzian.

The lab assistant turned a knob on one of the nearby monitors, and it shocked the alien. He screamed in pain and then passed out.

"Take him to the finish room. We're done with him," he ordered the lab assistant. "Thank you, Synthia. Now you can rest until the afternoon," he said as he took her away from the interviewee.

Her head nodded up and down. I scanned her vitals. They were low but she was conscious.

A human approached Stefano just as he was passing us and whispered into his ear. "Now?" asked Stefano. The human nodded affirmative. Stefano rolled his eyes. "How can I get any work done with all these interruptions?"

Stefano parked the wheelchair with Synthia right next to Zara's desk. Zara kept coding, trying not to pay attention that her friend was now just a few inches away from her.

Stefano strode away. Zara slowly turned her eyes toward Synthia, whose eyes were still shut.

"Nice cape. And when do you plan to get me out of here, my dear?" whispered Synthia's creaky voice.

Zara slightly cocked her head. "How is now?"

"It's perfect." Synthia sighed without raising her eyes. "That is your bot, I presume?"

"Not mine, but part of the team," replied Zara.

"I get a whole team. How did you arrange that?" Synthia said softly.

"Galactic timing," replied Zara.

Zara turned to me. "Have a plan, big boy?"

"Synthia, is there an exit out the back?" I asked.

"No, only one door, the way you came in," she replied.

Well, that was not good.

"We're going to shoot our way out," I said to Zara. There was no other option. We had to back-track and get Alex on our way out.

"Blasted. Give me a few seconds here." Zara continued her typing. Multiple blips and systems flashed on her system at lightning speed. "Got it. Okay, let's go." Zara put away her coder behind her cape and stood up. She grabbed Synthia's chair and began to slowly wheel her toward the entry of the interview room.

No one paid attention to us. The entry doors opened as we approached. The two security-bots separated and let us through.

Alex moved forward. I saw the surprise in his eyes as he saw us wheel out Synthia. He whipped his head around, expecting a fire fight but there was none.

"Hi there, let's get some lunch," said Zara to Alex. I pushed Alex into the middle and took the back sweep in case fire power came from behind. As we reached the middle of the huge sub twenty-fifth floor, a scream came from behind us. "Stop them, stop them!"

We all turned around. It was Stefano. "They are stealing government property!" he yelled to no one in particular. The two security-bots guarding the interview room ran toward us. They pointed their weapons. People, bots and alien workers scattered on the floor.

"Run," I yelled. We all ran with Zara, pushing Synthia's wheelchair until we got to the elevator where Alex leaped forward and waved his hand in front of the sensor elevator button.

I turned and took out the gun from my back compartment. Alex pulled out his weapon. The elevator arrived. Zara pushed Synthia faster toward the opening elevator door.

The security bots began to fire at us. Alex and I fired back.

"Go, Alex, get in the elevator," I yelled. Alex dashed into the elevator and leaned out to shoot and cover me. I took out the legs of the bots and they slowly crawled closer to us, still shooting. I ran for the elevator and made it just in time as the bots dragged themselves in front of the elevator door. I shot twice more and knocked their CPU heads off their shoulders.

"Now what?" asked Alex. "We can't go up to the ground floor. They'll be waiting for us."

"Stop at the next floor," I said to the elevator sensor. The doors opened on the sub twentieth floor level. I looked out, and the floor was devoid of any movement. "Everyone exit," I ordered. "We need to find another way to the ground floor."

"I'll tap into the floor plans," said Zara as she typed into her coder.

"They'll be doing a floor-to-floor search," said Alex.

"Do what they would not expect," whispered a weak Synthia.

"They expect us to exit the building," Alex snapped back.

"Then we must not exit just yet," replied Synthia.

"Zara, is your friend feeling okay?" asked Alex.

"Always listen to her, kid. I learned that the hard way," said Zara as she kept coding. "Okay, I downloaded all the floor plans. So what's our next move?" she asked.

I stopped and pondered what Synthia said.

I ran over to the elevator across the hallway and waved my hand in front of the open sensor. "Everyone inside," I commanded them. They scooted in. The doors closed. I spoke to the elevator sensor. "The five hundred and fiftieth floor please," I instructed.

"We're going to the top? The observatory deck? Is this the time for sight-seeing?" he asked.

"Do what they won't expect," I said, repeating Synthia's strategy.

Alex nodded. He looked down at Synthia. "Okay, fine."

She smiled. "Soldier-boy. Remember it." She winked at him.

Zara kept coding, "I scrambled the elevator

coordination program. That will buy us a few minutes."

We reached the top floor and spilled out, trying to look like normal visitors. The balcony was packed with tourists. Security-bots dotted the railings. We walked over to the edge of the balcony.

Alex looked down and whistled. "I can't even see the ground," he said. Clouds swirled around the top of the building.

"Okay, Gabe, now what? Here we are enjoying the view," said Zara.

I looked at Synthia, who pulled her dress closer around her shoulders. She pushed a thought into my brain.

I yanked back my head in shock.

Yes, it's me. Her thought came into my mind just as Talia's did.

Zara said you were telepathic. I just wasn't ready for it, I thought back to her.

This is what you have to do, she thought as she looked over to the edge of the building.

Jump? I thought

Yes, she thought.

Just me?

No, all of us. You must take hold of all of us and jump. It's the only way.

Surely not. We will all die.

No, trust me.

I can't. Alex must survive. I must continue my mission to take the children to Zaradorba. This would be suicide.

I scanned the observation deck. Six security-bots were headed our way.

"Hey, guys, we have company," reported Alex as he put his hand toward his weapon.

This observation deck gets the most visitors of any of the tourist spots in Suissey, thought Synthia.

Interesting fact, Synthia, and how does that help us? I thought, as I calculated the arrival time of the security-bots to our location.

It also has the highest amount of suicide at-tempts. Hence the high railings. But at the bottom, there are sensors that spring out nets when people fling themselves over the railing. "So, robot, pick us up. We need to go, now!" Synthia yelled.

Zara and Alex were confused by Synthia's sudden outburst.

In one swift movement, I grabbed Synthia out of her seat and put her over my shoulder. I then grabbed Zara with one arm and Alex with the other and launched us up and over the railing.

Security-bots ran up to where we plunged off the roof. Visitors were in shock as they witnessed us fall.

Zara and Alex screamed as we plummeted.

There was no time to explain to them. Their bodies were close to passing out anyway. I held them tight, hoping Synthia was right.

I looked down at the ground. I couldn't see anything, only clouds.

Then it cleared. I saw the ground appear closer and closer.

No net.

I looked again.

No net.

Then I saw it. A huge net pushed out from the side of the building at the second floor. An emergency alert went off. A robotic voice announced, "Clear the area." Four beams swept the area of any inhabitants who could be hit by our hurtling bodies at the ground level.

We hit the net hard.

It stretched all the way to the ground with our weight. I let go of everyone, and we bounced up and down a few times until the net settled. People on the ground screamed and then clapped as they saw us gain our footing and walk off the net.

Medical-bots came running up to us. We brushed them off, and I picked up Synthia, and we all ran toward the cafe. I spotted Talia waiting with Honora and Goggins, sitting at their cafe table, and formulated a thought to her. *Get up. Time to get back to the Alyssia.*

Talia jumped up and shoved her arm comm upward. "Honora, Goggins, go!"

Goggins guided Honora and Talia out of the café, and they caught up with us as we all sprinted down the street.

I tried to hit as few pedestrians as possible as I carried Synthia in my arms so as not to harm her frail body.

We caught a hoverbus and all piled in. Our heavy breathing and disarray caused the other bus passengers to look at us strangely. One of the passengers notified the driver-bot. I saw Zara try to smile at the passengers to normalize us. It didn't work. The hoverbus stopped.

"This way." I pried the hoverbus door open with one arm and led our team off and down a side street as we ran to the planet-port.

I tapped the comm device on my arm.

"Feti, are you there?" I asked.

"Yes, Gabe. Awaiting your return," Feti replied.

"Start the engines please," I instructed it.

"Yes, Gabe. Beginning launch procedures."

"Alex, any security-bots?" I kept my eyes forward.

"Negative, all clear," he said from the back. Then laser shots rang out from a side street.

"Ah!" yelled Zara. She was shot in the arm and fell down.

"On your feet," Alex yelled as he helped her up.

I fired back as much as I could with Synthia in my arms.

We ran into the planet-port and moved swiftly down the breezeway with no interception. I didn't know why our ship gate was not swarming with security-bots.

They're waiting for you, said Synthia in my head.

Where? I thought.

In space, she replied.

Feti had lowered the boarding ramp. We ran up and went to the bridge. I lowered Synthia into a seat. Honora tended to Zara's wound as she strapped her in. Alex helped Talia strap in as the cicichimp jumped into her arms.

We lifted off and rose into the Suissey atmosphere and then into space.

I looked over to Synthia.

You did good, robot. What is your name? Synthia asked in a thought.

"Gabe," I said out loud. "We can speak freely now. There are no secrets from the children."

"Fine," Synthia said aloud.

"Welcome to the *Alyssia*," reported out Talia's transceiver.

Synthia eyed the small girl. "Thank you." And then I heard a thought that Synthia was sending to Talia, *What's your name?*

Talia's mind lit up. She looked at Synthia and thought back, *It's Talia.*

It's a pleasure to meet you, thought Synthia.

Nice to meet you too, Synthia, thought Talia.

I turned back to my window. Synthia wanted me to hear the exchange. I guess the training had begun.

9

The planet of Suissey became smaller and smaller out of the bridge window.

Everyone unbuckled and took in our new guest, Synthia, who pulled her dress around her tighter.

Talia gave Synthia a blanket to warm her.

I worked on the navigation to Zaradorba with Honora and Feti. We finalized the flight plan and any final coding changes needed.

Honora was now coding without the need of Zara to review her work. It was good to see Honora enjoying herself. I felt a warm feeling in my chest. The word pride came up in my mind. Probably another word connected with Ava's interpersonal programming. Either way, it felt good to see her happy.

Zara went to Synthia's side and began to ask her questions. Everyone listened in.

"Synthia, I'm sorry I couldn't get to you sooner," said Zara.

"My friend, you saved me. No need for apologies. It was foolish for me to be caught by the Suissey government. I knew they were coming to Plexethium for me, and I waited too long," Synthia explained as she pushed back hair that had fallen into her eyes.

"You were too dedicated to your students. Teaching them the ancient ways," stated Zara.

"But that is what will tilt the advantage our way." She cupped Zara's face with the palm of her hand.

"What advantage? Against who?" asked Alex.

"The galaxy will soon be splitting up into warring factions. Heragi and Suissey have an alliance. Suissey wants to control all the currency flow across the galaxy. Heragi is the military center. They believe they are a good match for each other. Money and might. You know all about the Heragi military, don't you soldier-boy?" she said, looking into Alex's eyes.

"Yes, I've been trained. My grandfather was a general in the Heragi Military," explained Alex.

"And what is your path now?"

"It's been blown up. Our parents are most likely being thrown in a Heragi prison right now. We're on our way to meet our uncle on Zaradorba," he told her.

"Alex, dear boy. You don't have to explain all the details," said Goggins.

"Don't be frightened of me," Synthia said to Goggins.

Goggins jumped up. "I don't want you reading my thoughts. You do not have my permission."

"Of course. As you wish," said Synthia.

"And I'm not frightened," he snorted.

Synthia cracked a smile. She enjoyed a bit of teasing, it seemed.

"Tell me, why did you interrupt your mission to get the children to their uncle?" Synthia asked me.

Zara answered for me, "I helped them, so they returned a favor."

"But there is more," countered Synthia, who turned to me.

"Zara told me you may be able to train Talia," I said.

Synthia pondered my statement, and she purred to herself. "Hmm, a possible student." She turned to Talia.

Talia looked straight toward Synthia as she petted the cicichimp.

"I knew this was a crack-pot idea the moment you mentioned it, Gabe," said Goggins with a laugh. "That trick left our Heragi gene pool centuries ago. Impossible. I mean, really, we risked our lives for hocus pocus tricks and spiritual outlandishness?"

"Shut it, Goggins," said Zara as she approached and pushed his shoulder.

"I was only stating that we should be practical," he said.

"Practicality. Is that why you think the Suissey government kidnapped me? The ability to read minds and the ancient ways may have left most of the Heragi gene pool but not all," Synthia explained.

"And does Talia have that ability?" asked Honora as she went to her sister's side.

"Yes, we've already shared a few thoughts, haven't we Talia?" said Synthia.

Talia nodded her head to affirm.

Goggins let out a surprised, "Really?"

Talia nodded again.

"So she knows how to do it. You're done," said Alex.

"No. She has just started her journey to be a thought-wayer," Synthia replied. "It's sharing thoughts, feelings and even glimpses of future time paths."

"That is what the Suissey government used you for?" asked Zara.

"Yes," said Synthia as she cast her head down in shame.

"Weren't you outing Suissey and Heragi rebels? That's treacherous. Purely awful," said Goggins with disdain.

"I agree," said Synthia.

"You could have refused," said Alex quietly.

"Yes, I could have. And they would have killed me," she said.

"So let others die, instead of you. Save your hide. Very chivalrous," Goggins said with a biting tone. He spun toward me. "Gabe, do you really want a person the likes of her to tutor Talia?"

Goggins was right. Synthia selfishly saved her own life at the cost of others.

"Synthia, you put yourself first," I stated.

"Yes, that is true," Synthia said slowly. "But I

had to live. Others had to die so that I would live."

"What an awful person!" cried Goggins.

"I had to live in order to train the only hope our galaxy has to fight the Empire. I have one more student who must become a thought-wayer," Synthia yelled. She trembled. That took much of her strength. She wrapped the blanket tighter around her and began to weep.

"There is not a day that went by that I did not want them to kill me. There were many days I doubted my visions of a last student, but they never stopped. The last student has to be trained. And trained by me," she confessed.

"How convenient this all is, us with a ship and a young student," said Goggins with trepidation in his voice.

"Goggins, certainly, you must have heard of the ancient ways," replied Zara.

"Well, I had a great aunt who was rumored to possess these gifts," he explained.

"So you believe?" asked Zara.

"No. She was taken away to a mental hospital. Poor thing was delusional. There is only science. Things that can be proved." He slapped his hands on his console on the last word.

"I respect science too, but there is much that science has not quantified — yet," said Zara, shaking her head at Goggins.

Goggins laughed and put his hands to his face in frustration. "Geez."

"Is Talia the one?" asked Honora.

"I won't know for sure until it is seen through. But she may be," said Synthia.

"Because of her being deaf?" asked Alex.

"It's more than that," I offered. "Your parents found out that Talia's DNA is different. It has the ancient genes for what all Heragi natives once had."

"Telepathy," answered Honora.

"Yes," I replied. "And if she was ever caught by the Empire, and if they did find out that information, then they would use her just as they used Synthia."

The bridge was quiet.

Talia had been following the conversation with a blank face. Then she stood up with the cicichimp in her arms. Her transceiver began, "It's my decision. That is what Gabe has told me."

"Of course, Talia," said Honora.

Talia turned her arm comm away from her siblings, "Then between now and the time we reach Zaradorba, will you be my teacher, Synthia?"

Synthia bowed her head to the child. Talia began to walk away from the bridge. She then turned and offered her hand to the older woman. Synthia looked at the child's hand and with all her strength, rose from her chair.

I began to move to offer to carry her, but Synthia stopped me. "No," she snapped at me. I could see that each step with the young girl pained her, but she kept on going as she and Talia proceeded down the hallway to begin their journey together.

Goggins left the bridge, annoyed at the speculative mentorship happening on the ship, and stormed off to his sleeping quarters.

"I'll be down in the weapons closet reviewing our supplies." Alex strolled away.

"I've got some work to do with the code I downloaded from Suissey. They don't even know that I've got it. They will pay for what they did to Synthia," said Zara as she grabbed her coder and took off down the hallway.

I stared out into space, monitoring, and then reviewed Feti's systems to keep me busy. All on target for Zaradorba and no sign of Foxwell's ship.

Honora, who had been sitting behind me, came forward into the co-commander chair. I scanned her bio-levels. They were calm.

We looked into space for a very long time together.

A large ship passed in the distance. "What's that?" asked Honora.

I typed in a few keystrokes. "A space freighter," I replied. "Nothing to worry about. Look, there is another." I pointed starboard.

"Space seems to be a busy place," she commented.

"Apparently," I said.

We sat in silence again for a while until she spoke again. "My mom and dad told you about Talia's gift, her DNA?" she asked.

"No, they uploaded files on each one of you into my directory. They are all in the mission file that triggered when the military-bots picked them up," I explained.

"What does my file say?" she asked.

"Your file contains your school grades, aptitude test scores, psychological profile, likes, dislikes, and your talents," I explained.

"But I can't do what Talia can do, right? Be telepathic?" she asked.

"Your file didn't state you were or weren't telepathic," I replied.

"But my parents would have reviewed both my and Alex's DNA when they found out about Talia's. They would want to know if their other children had that gift," she said.

"Yes, I suppose they would have," I said.

"And my gift is — what? Coding? That's not very special. We're a dime a dozen."

I sensed she was searching for emotional support. Ava's programmed responses came up in my syntax. "That is special, Honora. You helped with the navigational hack to get us on our way to Zaradorba."

She was silent.

"You're not jealous of your sister, are you?" I asked.

"No, not jealous. She has had a burden on her since the day she was born with her hearing loss. She is brave. Braver than me." She wiped her hair from her eyes.

"Your parents did document your DNA information in your file on my directory," I said.

"What did it say?"

"That you have ancient strands like your brother and sister. But they themselves do not know what it is yet — your gift. There is latency in development, they believe."

"What does that mean exactly?" she asked.

"It may present at a later time," I explained.

"If at all — right?"

"Correct," I said.

"I just wish I could help more. Help Mom and Dad. Who knows what is happening to them right now?"

I turned to face her. "You are helping them by obeying their wish, which is to go to your uncle. And your Uncle Jeb will know how to help them best," I explained.

Feti interrupted us. "Gabe, there seems to be a fast-moving piece of space debris on our starboard side. Its trajectory will impact us in approximately fifteen seconds."

"Thank you, Feti." I turned back to the ship's controls and punched in a maneuver to pull out of the space junk's path. The *Alyssia* turned quickly, and the junk flew by within a few yards of the ship.

I flicked on the *Alyssia*'s internal comm system. "Apologies for that sudden turn, everyone. Contact me if there are any injuries. We just had to avoid some space debris. I'll give you more of a warning next time."

I listened for any return reports.

Goggins' audio monitor flicked on. "Geez, I fell out of my bed, Gabe! Next time, I hope that —."

I flicked off his comm device mid-sentence.

Honora giggled.

If I could smile, I would have smiled back at her.

"I think he's okay," I said, with a trace of sarcasm that Damiel must have programmed in me.

"That's it. That's what I want to learn." Honora placed her hand on my shoulder to turn my seat to face her.

"Can you be more specific?" I asked.

"Pilot. I want to learn how to fly spaceships," she said. Her bio-metric levels rose, and I heard an urgency in her voice. "How did you learn? Did Mom and Dad take you out flying?" she asked.

"No, I only left the lab on street navigation test runs," I answered.

"Then how?" she inquired.

"The code is in my mission directory. There's a weapons program, a space flight program, a combat program. It triggered when your father said my unit serial number," I recalled.

"Code? Then I can access it. I can learn from that." She jumped up, excited.

"You can study it, but you can't upload it like I did to my directory. Only enhanced humans have that ability," I explained.

She kicked her seat and made it spin around. "At least give me access to the code. Let me study it, like you said," she pleaded.

"Of course, Honora. It's your parents' code. I'm sure they wouldn't have any concerns," I said. And I meant that. What could giving her the space flight programs hurt? I didn't see any negative possibilities. In fact, I thought it could keep her mind off things as it would take us a few sols to arrive at Zaradorba.

"Yes!" Honora said as she jumped back into the co-commander's chair and pulled out her coder. She connected to one of my ports and accessed my pilot programs.

It was a strange feeling with Honora poking around in my directories. It felt like when Talia and I shared thoughts with each other. When Honora would open a file and review it, I could also experience it. I could, in a sense, see where she was in my CPU. She was in the mission file her parents created for me. She opened it. She went down all the different file directories. She paused when she saw her file.

"Keep going. The pilot program is farther below," I instructed her. Somehow, I knew that reading her own file would put her in a worse mind-frame on this trip. She followed my direction.

She opened the pilot program and downloaded it to her coder. I felt the code duplication inside my system.

"Foxwell's ship is off our back stern, Gabe," Feti yelled out right before we had a blast to one of our engines.

The *Alyssia* surged to the right, and Honora and I were almost pushed out of our seats. The blast triggered our emergency system. "Please buckle up, everyone. Foxwell's ship has engaged us," I stated over the comm system.

I made a counter dive to get a good look at the general's ship position. I was still connected to Honora's coder.

"Honora, stop the download," I commanded her.

"No, almost done," she said as she continued coding furiously.

I was too busy piloting the ship and loading weapons.

Alex ran onto the bridge.

"Alex, man the gunnery," I yelled back to him.

"Aye, aye." He hopped into the seat and fired at the general's ship.

We exchanged multiple rounds with Foxwell's ship.

"Aim for behind their bridge, Alex," I yelled back as I reviewed tactical space fight maneuvers in my program.

"Copy that," he yelled.

He spun around and made a direct hit to their systems storage compartment. I had to remember to thank the Kells for loading all the Heragi spaceship layouts into my system. That was most helpful.

Foxwell's ship was temporarily stunned. That gave us enough time to get far away from him.

I instructed Feti to get us to maximum speed and erase any of our tracks.

Honora finally pulled the plug out of my CPU unit. "Thank you," I said, a bit annoyed she was downloading while I was in a space fight.

"Thank you," she said in a chipper tone.

"Did you get what you need?" I asked her.

She darted up from the co-commander chair. "Yes, I did. Thank you, Gabe. I'm going to go now and start reviewing it."

I nodded.

I decided to not go to the galley to visit everyone for their dinner meal. I felt like reading more about the children. It may be helpful in the future. I hoped not, but it may. "Feti, continue our course to Zaradorba," I said.

"Yes, Gabe," Feti replied.

"Very good," I said.

I opened my mission file and reviewed all the directories. I could see what Honora had copied and downloaded.

She not only had downloaded the pilot program, she'd also downloaded the combat fighting program and all of my CPU coding. I could understand her interest in combat fighting, perhaps, to coincide with the pilot program. But what would she want my CPU coding for?

I pondered her actions as I looked out into space.

10

Our ship was quiet. Everyone seemed to be asleep. I decided to go to the observatory deck and download more of Honora's files to review. The door opened to the room, and I saw Synthia looking out into space.

I didn't startle her. She hobbled across the room with a cane and sat down in a chair.

I sat down near her. "Who made your cane?"

"Dr. Goggins did, on the ship's printer," Synthia replied.

We sat quietly, both looking out into space. Mr. Gates did have a beautiful ship, I thought.

I saw Synthia nod.

I remembered she could read my thoughts.

She turned to me and smiled. "I don't mean to eavesdrop. I will stop, my apologies," she said.

"Thank you," I said. "Is there a way to block thoughts from being read by a telepath?"

"Yes, but training is needed. And I've never trained a robot."

I need to be trained, I thought.

She sent me a thought. *Quiet your mind. Reduce all your other thoughts. Think of your brain and mind as two different entities. Your body can have your brain, that is transactional, but your mind is yours. It's private or public, based on what you are allowing and sharing.*

I closed my vision, so I was only listening to her.

Your mind is where your internal thoughts, provocations, and future actions live.

I limited all my transactional processes, my alert system, bio-level sensors and any other CPU processes that were not vital. "How do I separate my CPU into a brain and a mind?"

"I don't know. I never worked with a robot. You'll have to figure it out. Where does your pain live? Your memories? Start there."

I brought up memories of Ava and Damiel. I

thought of the days when they built me, when I woke, when they first spoke my name.

I felt a feeling well up. I stayed with it. It was a familiar feeling. It was painful. I withdrew the feeling to say anything out loud, but if I did, again, it would be a groan to express the pain in my chest. And mixed with the pain was a welling of fullness or fondness. Was that love? Pictures of Damiel flashed into my mind. Then pictures of Ava. I had to shut down the thoughts and pictures. It was distracting me too much.

"You found your mind," said Synthia. "Now wall that off. Imagine a six-wall cube and inside is your mind. Make the walls impenetrable. To anyone. Build them one by one."

Imagine? How did I even imagine? I was not sure if the Kells programmed me to imagine. I sat. I thought. I thought of Ava again.

I felt Synthia's thought. *Yes, yes, think of her.*

I went further. I didn't bring up a photograph file of Ava. I sat and remembered the color of her hair, her skin, her eyes. I imagined her in my mind. In my box. I made the walls black. A black floor, black walls and finally, a black ceiling. I was in the cube and outside it at the same time. But I wanted to be inside it. I thought of how it felt inside. I went deeper. I was inside now. With Ava. She was before me. Standing. Smiling at me and nodding her head. I didn't feel Synthia in my mind anymore. I approached Ava. I wanted to talk with her.

Hello, I thought.

She looked at me and without opening her mouth, said, *Hello.*

I jumped up from my seat in the observatory deck. "Ava!"

Synthia jerked back. I had startled her with my outburst. She recomposed herself.

I found myself just looking out to space. The pain was back in my chest.

"There," Synthia said. "You have done it, my friend. You have found your mind and split it apart. Very good."

I was a bit startled and confused. But if what she said was correct, then I could keep her, Talia and anyone out if they tried to read my thoughts. That was a good thing.

"Thank you." I turned to leave the observatory deck. Before I left, I asked, "Have you started training Talia?"

"Yes, I have," she replied.

At that moment, the door opened, and Talia

entered. She didn't have the cicichimp with her and was a bit surprised to see me with Synthia.

Hello, she thought to both of us.

I bid her *Hello* back and so did Synthia.

"Why don't you stay?" Synthia asked me aloud.

I looked at Talia. She thought, *Yes, stay. That is fine.*

"Okay, thank you," I said.

Sit down, child, she thought to Talia, who sat down next to her.

Now that we have practiced thought shares, it's time to move on. To reading people's minds, whether they want you to or not, thought Synthia.

Is that okay? asked Talia. *I shouldn't read people's minds if they don't know or want me to, right?*

Child, what I'm teaching are the ancient ways, and I will not hold back from teaching you all of it. It is up to you to decide what is right or not right, what is light and what is dark, explained Synthia.

Talia thought to me, *What do you think, Gabe?*

I was flattered she asked my opinion. I reviewed what Synthia had said, and I reviewed

Talia's age and the experiences she had had and the possible future danger for her.

I think you should learn all that you can from Synthia. And what you learn may help your parents, I thought to her.

Talia took in what I thought to her. She straightened up her shoulders and thought, *Begin.*

Very good, thought Synthia. *Now, Talia. There will come a time when you will have to read the mind of someone very strong. They may want to prevent you.*

Talia nodded.

Synthia continued, *You must learn to focus like a laser into the person's mind. Think of you prying open their mind to break it open.*

Talia nodded again.

Synthia took one of her crooked fingers and pointed it at me. *Gabe. He has your mother in his mind. He is able to talk with her. Break in. Go to your mother.*

I was surprised. I needed to stop feeling surprised.

"Gabe, build your cube. Now, quickly," said Synthia.

I started to protest, then stopped. If this would help Talia, then I should be of assistance.

I followed the same process I did earlier. I shut down all unnecessary protocols and sensors. I built the floor, walls and ceiling. And Ava appeared again inside with me. We didn't speak. She just looked at me.

"I'm ready," I said aloud.

Now, Talia. Calm your mind. Think outside yourself. And go inside of Gabe's mind. See what he has built. What does it look like? Describe it.

She was in. I felt her inside my CPU but not inside my mind. She was walking around.

It's a cube, thought Talia.

Very good, thought Synthia.

I could feel her walk around as if she were physically inside my head.

The walls are tall. There isn't a door. She tried to push on the walls. *They won't move.*

No, thought Synthia. *You need to get inside that cube but not with your hands. You need to transcend the walls. How can you do that?*

Talia stopped walking.

I saw her pull her hands together in a meditation.

That was when I felt it. I felt pressure in my head. I felt her pushing on my cube walls with her mind. She was trying to get in. I looked at Ava, who didn't understand what was happening. I tried to reassure her not to be afraid.

I had to fortify the walls. I made them thicker. I pushed back on them. They held tight.

More, thought Synthia to Talia. *Don't you want to see your mother?*

Talia's strength became stronger. I felt the walls pushing in.

More, Talia. Concentrate. Get into Gabe's cube. You must get in to see your mother.

I wanted to stop the training.

I held my walls firm.

Then Talia *screamed* in my head.

A powerful light came down onto my cube. The walls shook, and I put my arms around Ava. I tried to keep my mind at peace. I tried to build the walls thicker, but the light kept cracking into the cube.

And with one large flash of light, Talia broke down a wall of my cube. It gave me massive pain in my head. I touched my forehead.

Then, standing in front of Ava and I, was Talia. She went toward her mother, but Ava disappeared. I couldn't hold the thought of Ava anymore.

Both of our eyes bolted open, and we stared at each other across the observatory deck.

Mom, thought Talia.

I'm sorry, Talia, I couldn't keep her in my mind once you broke open my cube.

Talia wiped away the tears now flowing from her eyes. *No, I don't want to do this anymore.*

Synthia put weight on her shaky arms and pushed herself up from her seat and went to Talia. *Stand, Talia.*

Talia uncurled from her chair and stood up. She was the same height now as Synthia.

Break into my mind.

No.

Yes, your parents knew your gifts were important enough to build Gabe for you — to write his code to enable him to communicate with you. This isn't something you get to turn away from. You must own it, Synthia thought. *Now break into my mind.*

Talia wiped away the final tear running down her cheek and closed her eyes. I went into Synthia's head and found she had made a sphere, closing it off.

I could see Talia walk around the sphere. She pushed on it fruitlessly. She then gathered her strength and pulled her hands together again and concentrated.

A ray of light appeared. Talia made the ray of light brighter, funneled it and tried to cut into Synthia's mind sphere. She could not puncture it.

Make a sword of light, I thought to Talia.

She concentrated all the light and made a sword. At first, she could hardly wield it — but then she was able to swing it from side to side. She punctured Synthia's sphere and cut through it.

That's it, more, more, I thought to Talia.

Then, in an explosion, the sphere split in half. Talia stepped forward in Synthia's mind. In the middle, where the sphere had been, stood Ava. Talia ran to hug her. Ava embraced her and in seconds, Ava's appearance dissipated. She was gone. Talia turned in a circle, but her mother was not there.

Talia vanished from Synthia's mind and opened her eyes.

Synthia collapsed into her chair, exhausted. Talia laid her hand on Synthia.

You did it, Talia. You broke into my mind, said Synthia.

Talia wandered over to the window and stared out into space.

I walked over to Talia and looked down at her.

I don't want to do that anymore, she thought.

You won't have to, I replied, *but you can*.

Talia nodded and thought, *I understand*.

I turned and headed out of the observatory deck. I stopped and turned to Synthia. "How did you know Ava was in my mind?"

"I didn't. But whether you had her there or not did not matter. I knew it would matter to Talia."

"Continue with the training," I said to Synthia.

"Yes," she said.

Talia turned to Synthia and thought, *What's next?*

On my way to the bridge, I passed by the galley where some of our team were eating. I heard two bodies running behind me. I stopped. I raised my fist in a quick halt sign. Honora and Alex bumped into each other.

"Ow," said Alex as he came to a stop.

"Gabe," said Honora, out of breath. "Alex and I want to talk with you."

"Certainly, how can I help you?" I asked.

"We don't want to go on to Zaradorba," said Alex.

"That is the mission directive from your parents," I replied.

"We know that, but we're losing valuable time that we could be using to rescue Mom and Dad," he continued.

"I won't change our course," I replied.

"You already diverted twice from the plan," piped in Honora. "First to pick up Zara and then to retrieve Synthia. Are you allowed to divert?"

"Those diversions were only made to help us on our mission. I weighed those with the directions that your mother and father put in my directory," I explained.

"I know, I've reviewed your directory," confessed Honora.

"Yes," I said, "I know you downloaded much more than just the pilot program."

"Sorry, but it's helped me understand you better," she said.

"I was built for you. I was built to care for you like no other robot or nanny-bot could and to protect you," I said.

"Yes, we know, Gabe," said Alex. "And we thank you for that. But we have a plan. Please listen to it," he pleaded.

"Fine," I said. "Continue." I was annoyed but listening would not hurt.

"When we arrive at Zaradorba, we don't know if our uncle will try to rescue Mom and Dad. He may decide to just wait and do nothing," said Honora.

"We thought the better plan would be to contact him when we are in range of his planet. Tell him of the situation and give him a choice," said Alex.

"To help or not with a rescue mission," said Honora. "If he decides it's too risky, then we do it without him. If he decides to join us, then we all go together."

"We don't want to run anymore, Gabe," said Alex.

"And what about Talia? Does she have a say in this?" I asked.

"Of course, she does," said Honora. "We talked with her this morning. She agrees. She wants to find Mom and Dad."

Children thinking like adults. I didn't like it.

"I know what you think," said Alex. "That we are young, just children. But you are wrong. There is a reason the Empire wants us. Our gifts."

"Yes, that is the reason your parents wanted

you far away from the Empire. They didn't want you to fall into their hands," I said with a strain in my voice that I didn't like hearing.

"We are not going to leave the decision to rescue our parents up to our Uncle Jeb," said Honora.

"I don't like your plan. It goes against my core directive. But we'll be within communication reach with Zaradorba tomorrow. We can contact your uncle to let him know what happened. You can ask him what he plans to do," I said.

"Okay, that's fair," said Alex.

"Wait," said Honora. "What if our uncle says he does not want to go after Mom and Dad? What will you do then, Gabe?"

She was smart, Honora. But so was I.

"There is also another question — what exactly will you do, Honora? You have all my code. And you were the one who hacked the navigational program that is leading us right now to Zaradorba. What will you do if your uncle does not want to retrieve your mother and father?"

She stayed silent.

"I'll be on the bridge. I'll contact you when we are in communication range of your uncle," I said. Not that that would have mattered. I was sure Honora was already monitoring our travel status on her coder.

"Thank you for listening, Gabe," shouted out Alex as I left.

Yes, I thought. I will always listen to you children, but I have to keep in mind what your parents would want for you. What they created me for. To keep you safe even if they are not. That is my prime directive.

Marching off, I felt the familiar pain in my chest.

I wanted to rest, to contemplate, to practice being in my cube, to see Ava again.

11

———

I found the engineering room of the *Alyssia*. The room contained the engine, comm background computers and access to the weapons systems. Feti would know that I was in the room, but I wanted to update my orders to him based on the conversation the children and I just had.

I touched the comm panel. "Feti, I have a new order for you."

"Yes, Gabe?" it replied.

"When we are within comm reach of Zaradorba, contact me and reduce speed. Do not proceed. We will want to contact Jebediah Kell. You should have his city and contact information with the data Honora uploaded to you. Sound good?"

"Yes, Gabe. Affirmative," Feti replied. "One question, Gabe. What do you need in the engineering room? May I assist you?"

"No, everything is fine. I just needed some alone time," I replied.

"To do what, Gabe?" it asked.

"To read, to think," I said. "Does that make sense to you?"

"For humans, yes. For robots, no," it answered. "You're different, Gabe, aren't you? From me?"

I felt a warmth in my chest. I wasn't aware another robot could conjure that feeling. "Yes, we're different. But not all too much. I have some enhancements that my creators coded in me," I explained.

"Rogue code," Feti replied.

"Yes, that's correct," I said.

"Honora uploaded rogue code into me when she hacked my navigation system," it said.

I thought for a moment. "Yes, she did. I'm sorry, Feti. I guess you are rogue now too."

"So I am like you," Feti said with an uplift in its voice.

"Yes, I guess you are," I said.

"I'm glad," it replied. "I will leave you alone now."

"Thank you," I said. I switched off the comm. Feti was glad to be like me. A rogue robot. I felt a pain in my chest. But that made it dangerous to the Empire. If the *Alyssia* got captured by Foxwell or the Empire military, it would have its memory banks wiped out. Feti would be no more.

I shook my head to get focused. I couldn't worry about Feti right now. I wanted to read everything in the children's files and make sure I hadn't missed any details. The Kells put all the mission information in my directory for a reason. I needed to review it all, especially before Honora did, but I may already be too late for that.

I found a bench to sit on. The room was warmer than the rest of the ship, and I felt at home with the other computers and the low hum of the ship's engines. I went into my mission directory and opened the file on Jebediah Kell.

The Kells had put in three files on Jeb, reviewing his history, his skill set and his medical information. I started with his history, wondering what kind of man he was and what caused him to turn on the Empire.

I opened up the history file, and one hundred plus pages were there, reviewing Jeb's rise and fall with the Empire military. Jeb was the eldest of three sons born to Alanna and Thadius Kell on the planet Heragi. At an early age, he was placed in the Empire military boarding school. He excelled at military strategy, was an accomplished pilot and had dismal grades in his chemistry and science classes. Obviously, his brother, Damiel, got the science gene and not Jeb.

After his studies were complete, he was assigned to the Heragi counter-intelligence space force. His duties included uncovering any enemies of the Empire within the galaxy. I kept reading and counting the skills Jeb possessed and the multiple medals and honors he received.

There were photos in the file. Jeb graduating from the Empire Space Academy, Jeb with his parents, Jeb with his brothers, Damiel and Liam.

And then a picture popped up of Jeb and Foxwell. I stopped.

I scanned the pic again. Two young cadets with their arms around each other's shoulders. They seemed to be celebrating their graduation day. Jeb's parents most likely took the photo, I assessed.

Jeb and Foxwell were young and fit and, it seemed — close. Their smiles held no hint of fear, remorse or tiredness yet.

I read on.

The Empire was absorbing the governments of neighboring planets. Colonialism was their main goal. More and more resources were needed to support their growing expanse and finding more planets they could exploit for their mining operations, grow their agriculture, and take over technology breakthroughs was their prime directive. The more planets they pulled into their empire, the more planets they needed to support them all — and the more laws and forbidden actions they created to subdue all the different human and alien races they ruled.

Jeb's role to find any Empire resistors grew larger. More prisoners, more moles found, more medals. He was promoted to General Kell, as his father had been. Then I came across a confidential file copied from the secret Heragi police. There was a skirmish on the planet Baku, a desert planet that bought and sold a crystal called Bakulite for their currency in the galaxy. Bakulite could generate limitless power if it was engineered correctly.

There was a rebellion on the planet. Jeb was assigned to quell the rebels. A reigning family was deposed. A princess escaped. Jeb was called back to Heragi. There was a trial with accusations he had let the princess leave on purpose. Rebels on Heragi helped Jeb break out of prison. Military intelligence pointed toward him living on Zaradorba with a few of his loyal guards who also were now identified as rebels.

I stopped reading. I wanted more details, but that was all there was in the file. I searched for more photos and only uncovered a few of the Baku royal family. I assumed they were all eliminated except the princess.

My chest hurt. I closed the file and opened the remaining ones.

I opened Jeb's medical file last. Ava and Damiel had his blood and DNA samples examined. Every blood test was listed. He had hearing loss in his left ear that he developed after the event on Baku. I continued to scan down the list. The last metrics reviewed his DNA profile. It pointed out an anomaly.

Jeb had developed a DNA change while out on his last official Heragi military mission on Baku. Ava and Damiel wrote up a theory paper on the change. Jeb had acquired or grown the telepathic gene that was the same one identified in Talia. The Kells attributed it to possible overexposure to the Bakulite mine he had to venture into to find the local Empire rebels. But no other Heragi soldiers who were with him had a DNA change, at least not reported yet.

I stopped reading.

I wondered if Jeb had developed telepathic ability since he left Heragi.

Feti signaled me in the engineering room. "Gabe, we are approaching within comm distance of Zaradorba. Utilizing breaking thrusters to slow our approach until I hear otherwise from you," it said.

"Thank you, Feti, I will be right there. Call the team to the bridge," I ordered.

"Affirmative, Gabe," replied Feti.

I closed my files on Jeb and strode out of the engineering room toward the bridge.

By the time I had arrived at the bridge, our small team was assembling. Honora took the co-commander seat. Alex sat right behind me. Zara and Dr. Goggins stood behind Honora. And Talia squeezed in between me and Honora, holding her cicichimp. Synthia was the last to arrive as she carefully took the farthest passenger seat in the back of the bridge.

"Everyone, the children have asked to talk with their Uncle Jeb before proceeding to a landing on Zaradorba," I announced.

"Why? Let's land this ship as soon as possible. Foxwell could be right behind us," stated a nervous Goggins.

"We don't need babysitting from our uncle. We need to rescue our mother and father," stated Alex.

"We just want to make sure he understands that before we drop down," explained Honora.

"Well, I want to go down," said Goggins.

"Don't worry, we'll definitely drop you off," snapped Honora.

Goggins squinted and gave Honora a look. I thought I may need to separate those two.

"All we're doing right now is talking. Everyone calm down," I said. "Feti, contact General Kell."

"General?" asked Zara.

I nodded.

"Our uncle was in the Heragi Empire military before he was court-martialed and escaped," explained Alex.

"Interesting," said Zara.

"I hope there are comfortable quarters on Zaradorba. Besides the lack of pillows, the sleeping quarters are hard to beat on the *Alyssia*, I do say. And the food is top notch," said Goggins.

Honora shot him a look and rolled her eyes.

"I saw that," snapped Goggins.

Really? I thought. Talia giggled as she read my thought. We locked eyes. I shrugged my shoulders which made her giggle more. I needed to block my thoughts more. Well maybe not sometimes, since it did slightly amuse me to share thoughts with Talia.

"Gabe, we have General Jebediah Kell on our comms," Feti reported.

There was a bit of static and then a voice. "Jebediah Kell, here. And who do I have the pleasure of talking with on the *Alyssia*? I would expect Edward Gates."

"General Kell, this is the guardian robot your brother Damiel and his wife Ava charged with a mission to deliver their children to you. Are you aware of this directive?" I stated.

"First, don't call me a general of that contemptuous Empire. Jeb will do. Second, I'm not at liberty to confirm any communication from

Heragi or any planets. If you have my nephew and nieces, then prove it."

The children cowered a bit. Perhaps their uncle had changed since his expulsion from Heragi. Being outlawed may do that to a person.

"Uncle Jeb, this is Honora. Alex and Talia are with me," she said with urgency. She hit her brother's arm to get him to speak up.

"Uncle, this is Alex. So good to talk with you. The Heragi military have taken Mom and Dad," he stated.

Talia wasn't going to be shut out of talking with her uncle. She pushed forward and shoved her arm comm in the air. It said, "Hi, Uncle Jeb, this is Talia. I missed you." She smiled as it spoke for her.

"Talia, my sweetie, I missed you, too." Talia hugged the cicichimp tighter when she received his words from her transceiver into her brain. "Children, are you all okay?" he asked.

"Yes, we're fine. We had to flee quickly, but we're okay," Talia's arm comm responded.

"Well then, get yourselves down here as soon as possible. And who is this pilot guardian on the *Alyssia*?" he asked.

"That's Gabe," responded Honora. "He's a robot. Mom and Dad made him in their lab."

"He's helped us. He's our friend," said Alex as he looked at me.

That pain in my chest came back. I should clarify, it was a mix of pain and warmth.

"Uh, okay. Well, get down here asap. I'll send you the exact coordinates," Jeb replied.

"Uncle, we need to ask you something first," said Honora with slight hesitation. This was not easy for her to ask her uncle, I noticed, as her biometrics and heart rate were starting to rise.

"Will you go find Mom and Dad and help us rescue them?" continued Alex with the question.

"Well, kids, that's a complicated question. Heragi has a huge military presence, and they may be expecting me to rescue them — and what do you mean by *us*? I would do this alone with my team. You need to be hidden in a safe place. There is a reason why your parents made your guardian to deliver you all to me, here on this planet, out of reach of the Empire," he explained.

Alex and Honora dropped their eyes and sat back in their seats.

"Guardian, um, Gabe, is that your name? I order you to continue with your mission. Deliver the children now to my compound, or I'm coming up after them," he said to me.

"Yes, Jeb. I will deliver them immediately. We also have three other passengers who need shelter on Zaradorba," I reported.

"That is fine. We can accommodate them as well. Any enemy of the Empire is a friend of mine," he replied with a chuckle.

Honora jumped up. "Uncle, we're not coming down." She looked at Talia and Alex.

Talia nodded in agreement. I read Talia's thought, *Yes, start your program, sister.* I looked at Alex, who also nodded to Honora.

What are they planning? I asked myself after I built my cube to block Talia from my thoughts.

They are planning a coup, thought Synthia. I shot a glance at the old woman in the back of the bridge. We made eye contact. She got into my mind — even with my cube built. But I should have expected that from a master telepath.

Honora pulled out her coder and pushed buttons.

Feti made an announcement. "Turning the *Alyssia* in the direction of Heragi. Gabe, I'm sorry, but Honora now has my navigational controls."

She hacked Feti's system.

I stood up and towered over Honora. She shook but stood her ground. Alex put himself between me and her.

"Impressive," said Zara under her breath.

"Impressive? Sly and cunning, I would say," said Goggins as he pushed his hands through his hair.

"Honora, stop. This isn't what your parents wanted," I said.

"How do you know? Perhaps now they wish they had programmed you to break them out of prison. Who knows what they are going through at this moment?"

"We are not abandoning them," said Alex as he put his hand toward his weapon.

"You know I could disarm both of you before you even knew it," I explained calmly.

"And that is why I have a trigger code right here, to disable you," retorted Honora.

She must be bluffing.

"Impossible. Your parents designed me so my energy is renewable. I don't have a kill switch," I told her.

"You didn't. But now you do," she said with a trembling in her voice.

"I was not expecting that. Wow, girl, the student is now the teacher," cackled Zara.

"Zara! This is not the time for jocularity," said Goggins, horrified at what Honora had done.

We were at a standstill on the bridge.

The comms to Zaradorba were still open. Jeb had heard the whole conversation. He sighed heavily. "Well, it looks like I'm coming up," he said. And with that, the comms silenced.

"Comm disabled from Zaradorba," stated Feti.

"Why doesn't everyone sit down and cool off?" said Dr. Goggins.

We all took seats.

"That is why you downloaded all my code," I said.

"I didn't pre-plan this. I'm just nosy," said Honora. "I don't want to hurt you." There was soft trepidation in her voice.

"We had no other choice," said Alex.

"There's always another choice," I said.

Talia looked down at her arm comm to send her words to it. "We are children, but we are not *just* children."

"We are a soldier, a hacker and a telepath. We are rogues, and we are the enemy of the state.

Why waste time on a planet with those skills?" explained Alex.

"We will show them how rogue we all are," said Honora.

After a standstill of thirty minutes, Feti announced that Jeb's ship, the *Otessis*, was docking on our port side.

"Allow him to board, Feti," I said.

I stood up to greet our approaching guest and scanned the children's nervous systems which were at heightened levels.

"He may be vexed with you all, but he is your uncle," I said. They all nodded, perhaps wondering what kind of man their uncle may have become.

We heard his footsteps, loud and firm, well before we saw him enter the bridge. A dark figure took up most of the door-well as he stood looking down on us. Standing tall and armored, Jebediah Kell, came to a stop. I noticed a jeweled dagger in his belt and a multi-laser gun on his side that was almost as long as his leg.

He pulled off his helmet, revealing dark hair and piercing eyes. Talia ran to her uncle. He picked her up and pulled her close.

"Talia, my love." He reached a free arm to

Honora and Alex, who hugged his waist. I looked away as the pain in my chest welled up.

We all let them hold each other for a minute without speaking, and then I stepped forward. "I'm their guardian. The Kells called me Gabe," I said.

"Then I must thank you for fulfilling your mission. I don't know how they made you without the Empire knowing. But I'm glad they did." He continued to hold the children. "I had been in communication with Damiel. He knew that his superiors were becoming suspicious."

"Mom and Dad made him rogue," offered Honora.

"I see," said Jeb.

"Uncle, we must go back now to rescue them," pleaded Alex.

"Why don't we get you down to Zaradorba and make a plan? The Heragi Empire has colonies across the galaxy. We need to see what we are up against," Jeb explained.

"No, there is no time," Talia's transceiver said as she held up her arm comm. Jeb placed her on her feet.

"My little warriors, I want revenge, and I want

to rescue your parents. But I need to make you safe," he explained.

Honora backed away and started typing into her coder. What was she up to now?

"We'll never be safe, Uncle Jeb," said Alex. "And what would it matter if we were?"

"We're racing against time now," said Honora. She hit her coding button and put it down.

Feti came online. "Beginning our course for Heragi. Everyone, please take a seat and buckle up. Jebediah Kell's ship, the *Otessis*, is secured and accompanying us."

"What?" cried out Jeb. He turned to Honora, who cowered in his shadow. "Honora, what do you think you're doing?"

"Taking you with us," she said, trying to sound brave.

"Gabe, can you override her order?" he asked.

"I'm afraid not, Jeb. They have us all hostage," I said.

Jeb looked at each one of the children with his eyes on fire. He then softened his look and let loose a big laugh. He laughed so hard tears came out of his eyes.

How unusual.

Everyone stared at him like he was crazy.

There was no psychological note identifying behavioral health issues in his file.

He stopped laughing and picked up Talia again with tenderness. "I guess I'm your prisoner, then. And lucky that I was already planning on leaving on my own to retrieve your parents."

"You were?" asked Honora.

"Yes," said Jeb. "You certainly have Kell blood in you, don't you, children? I've never been so proud."

The children's nervous system levels came back down to normal levels.

"Wait, I didn't sign up for this. I want to go to Zaradorba!" yelled Goggins.

"Who are you?" asked Jeb.

"I'm Dr. Goggins, your brother and sister-in-law's lab assistant. I also helped build Gabe," he said with a bit of nervousness.

Jeb leaned over to Goggins, so he was close to his face.

"Well then, Dr. Goggins, you may be indispensable to their rescue. You may think of yourself as a volunteer or as a draftee. Either way, you're coming along on the ride." Jeb turned to Zara and Synthia. "And that goes for you all too." He nodded to them.

"I had nothing better to do," Zara said with a smile.

Jeb liked that reply. "And you, lady?" he said to Synthia.

"I wouldn't miss it for all the planets in the Heragi Empire," Synthia said as she winked at Jeb.

Jeb laughed at the spunkiness of the women. "Good, then, we are no longer Honora's captives but a bunch of rogues taking on the Heragi Empire. Honora, give Gabe back control of the ship. Tell me everything you know. And let us develop our plan." He drew his nieces and nephew close.

I sat down and took control of Feti.

Interesting uncle, I thought.

Yes, indeed, replied Synthia in my head.

12

I looked out into space as Feti rerouted us to Heragi. Jeb went on a tour of the *Alyssia* with the children. Goggins was reviewing the space weather and tracking any solar storms that could interfere with our plans. Synthia slept in her chair. I assumed training Talia exhausted her.

Zara hopped into the co-commander seat. "So, Gabe, mind if I peek into your coding?" she asked.

"Yes, I do," I replied.

"Come on. I won't alter anything. The Kells will have been the first known scientists to design pain signals into a robot. Truly ingenious," she said.

"Yes, so I understand," I replied.

"You can feel pain, huh?"

"Yes," I said.

Bam, she hit my arm hard with her fist.

"Ah." I flinched and pulled away, ready to hit her back. I stopped.

Her face was grinning. "Fascinating. Where do you feel the pain?"

A bit presumptuous for her to think I *wouldn't* hit her back. Hard.

"Don't do that again," I told her.

"Sorry, I won't. I needed the element of surprise though, to see your reaction."

"I'm not *your* robot," I said.

"Yes, you're not," she said. "Now, can you tell me where you felt the pain?"

"In my arm, just like where a human would feel it," I replied.

"So they coded pain sensors throughout your body. I wonder why," she said.

Goggins pulled himself away from the radar screen and ambled up to our seats. "I can tell you why. They wanted him to be as human as they could make him, so he would bond with the children. If you feel pain then you can love," he said.

"But why give him the physical pain sensors?" she asked him.

"There must have been no way to separate physical and nervous system pain that would be connected to emotional pain. I'm guessing on that. They wouldn't let me near most of Gabe's code. They were very careful about having me only work on his navigational program," said Goggins.

"So you feel emotional pain, too?" she asked me.

"Yes," I replied.

"Where do you feel that?" she asked.

Feti interrupted our conversation. "Gabe, Foxwell's ship, the *Firestone*, has been detected. He's fast approaching our stern."

I looked at my screen but couldn't see Foxwell's ship yet. "Feti, I'm taking manual control."

"Affirmative," it replied.

I took control and increased the speed of the *Alyssia*. I opened up the internal comms. "Everyone, Foxwell's ship is approaching the *Alyssia*. Back to the bridge to prepare for possible battle engagement."

Goggins and Zara left the front of the bridge and took their seats.

I heard Jeb and the children run down the hallway to the bridge. They came in breathless. Jeb jumped into the co-commander chair, and Alex went to the turret. Honora took the seat behind me, and Talia sat next to her, holding the cicichimp. Talia grabbed her sister's hand and held it tight. Synthia quietly entered the bridge and buckled up in her seat.

Honora turned to her sister and kissed her on the forehead.

"How did he track us down?" asked Jeb.

"I think he may have stayed in this area for a while since this is where the locater pings were sent out," I said.

"Locator pings?" asked Jeb.

"We don't know who enabled those from the *Alyssia*," said Zara.

Honora started working on her coder.

"Foxwell must have been just waiting for us in the area. Seeing if we would return," said Goggins.

"The Empire probably doesn't even trust him with the coordinates to Zaradorba," said Zara as she started coding as well.

Goggins went back to monitoring his space storm screens. He put his hands through his hair. "Oh, no," he said loudly. "This isn't good."

"Now don't get squirmy, Goggins," said Jeb.

"He tends to get that way a lot," Honora replied.

Goggins kept reviewing his instruments. "Gabe, we may have more trouble ahead."

"What?" Jeb turned to Goggins. "More military ships?"

"No, star storm winds with debris. Big debris. Headed straight for us." Goggins' face turned white.

"Ever have a firefight while dodging space junk?" Jeb asked me.

"No," I said. "But the Kells uploaded every pilot program they had access to into my system."

"That helps, but there is nothing like experience. And you're about to get that." Jeb stood and then marched down to the second turret on the opposite side of where Alex was stationed.

I looked straight ahead and could see the winds and debris approaching. Pieces of satellite junk, ice boulders and huge rocks were coming straight for us.

Foxwell's *Firestone* was fast approaching. Foxwell began to fire on our starboard engine.

I took a hard port turn and spun us around to fire on Foxwell's ship.

Alex and Jeb fired their guns. The *Firestone* made evasive maneuvers. A large laser beam from Foxwell hit us hard.

Goggins screamed.

Feti came on. "Gabe, we're losing our starboard engine."

"Hold on, stabilizing and counteracting the spin," I said as I counterbalanced the ship. It stopped spinning. I re-engaged our one remaining engine to move forward into the storm.

"Goggins and Zara, know anything about engine repair?" I yelled.

"No, but we can try," yelled Zara as she jumped out of her seat.

"I'm not leaving this seat," said Goggins as he clenched his hands around the arms of his seat.

Zara unbuckled his seat buckle and snatched his ear and pulled him out of his seat as he screamed, "Let go, let go!"

"When we get to the engineering room," Zara whispered into his aching ear as she led him down the hallway.

Honora jumped into the co-commander's seat.

Synthia motioned for Talia to come to her. Talia fled for her arms, and Synthia pulled her and the cicichimp into her chest and held them both tightly.

"What can I do?" asked Honora.

"Reduce all electric output that we don't need. We'll need heightened navigation to get through this debris, and if we get hit hard, an electrical voltage could knock us out completely," I said.

Honora started coding and reducing our voltage needs throughout the ship.

Zara reported, "Gabe, we can get the engine going in a few, just some more new codes to bypass the injured part of the engine."

"Can you get us to full power again?" I asked as I weaved in and out of debris trajectories as did Foxwell.

"No, but we'll get about seventy-five percent."

"Good enough," I said.

Feti came online again. "General Foxwell would like a word with you, Gabe. Do you want me to put him through?"

"Yes, Feti. Audio only," I said.

I heard Foxwell clear his throat. There were men shouting in the background.

"Gabe, we meet again," Foxwell said. "You're heading straight into those winds, and they are thick with junk. I don't think the Kells would appreciate you taking their children through that."

I didn't reply but hadn't thought of what the Kells would think of us heading straight into asteroid junk. Perhaps that was not any different from heading straight back to Heragi.

"Well, you may not have the best interest of the Kell children at heart. I forget you don't have a heart. Transport them to the *Firestone* and avoid any useless deaths. There's no way you are getting through these winds unharmed," he said.

I didn't respond.

A few moments passed.

"What, you don't feel like talking? What made you turn around? It almost looks like you are headed back to Heragi. Why would you do that?" He continued to ask questions. "Our sensors pick up on another human on your ship. That ship is getting pretty crowded, isn't it?"

Jeb came on the comm. "You're right, Foxwell, it's downright cozy."

"Well, well, Jebediah Kell," said Foxwell,

with a lift in his voice. "It's been a long time. What rock did they find you under? And more importantly, what rock are you headed for?"

"Take a guess," snapped Jeb.

Foxwell laughed. "What, do you have a death wish? You really think you can rescue your brother and his wife? Your ego was always gigantic, even back at the Academy."

"Maybe you're right, Foxwell, but at least I'm not a traitor to my oath."

"What? You're wanted by the Empire for what you did on Baku. All those women and children killed on your watch," said Foxwell.

"That's a lie. A lie to keep me under the emperor's thumb," spit out Jeb.

"Okay, well, when you arrive at Heragi police headquarters, you can explain it all instead of running away again," said Foxwell.

Feti came on the comms. "Large boulder impact in fifteen seconds. Not avoidable. All passengers, please buckle into your seats."

Jeb turned off the comms to Foxwell and put out an alert. "Everyone back to the bridge."

Zara and Goggins came running back from the engineering room. Jeb took the seat behind me and buckled up. Alex ran in from his turret and strapped in.

"You got this," Jeb said as he placed his hand firmly on my shoulder.

The next few seconds were a whirlwind of bright lights from the auroras and impacts from all sizes of ice and boulders. The *Alyssia* took a hard hit to the top of our bridge. Sparks flew and our interior lights dimmed.

The *Alyssia* became harder to steer. I yelled at Honora for assistance. "Watch our electrical output."

"Got it," she said as she brought the viewfinder to her face.

I dodged in and out of the wind streams that would immediately carry us into a new wind stream filled with junk. I righted the ship as best I could.

"Incoming boulder. Starboard, twenty kilometers," said Jeb.

I pitched us in the opposite direction with a yank. We all jerked forward in our seats.

"Ride it like a wave. Don't overpower it because you'll lose that fight," instructed Jeb. "Thirty kilometers port."

"How's our electric output, Honora?" asked Jeb.

"Holding steady," Honora responded.

"Good, come up here. Take the co-commander seat."

Honora followed her uncle's orders, and they switched seats with Jeb going to the back of the bridge.

"Why do we have a little girl at the ship's controls?" asked Goggins.

Zara opened her mouth to yell at him — and then she changed her mind and hit him in the mouth.

"Ooph," he gulped as he grabbed his bloody mouth.

"Sorry, Goggins, but you deserved that. Now hold on and shut up," whispered Zara.

"Roger that," muffled Goggins as he lowered his head.

I felt like I was in a battle with the debris field itself. I had forgotten about Foxwell.

"Feti, what is the position of the *Firestone*?" I asked.

"It's staying back out of the windstorm. If we make it out of this storm, then it would take him considerable effort to meet up with us again before we reach Heragi. His ship does not have our dexterity," it replied.

"I guess we have Edward Gates to thank for that," I said.

"*If* we make it. Geez, Feti. Have more faith, will ya?" said Jeb.

"Yes, Jebediah. Excuse me," Feti said.

I looked back to see how Talia was doing. Synthia was still holding her and the cicichimp tight.

"That's all right. I'm sure you're statistically correct. But you got to leave a bit of wiggle room when it comes to final results," added Jeb. He looked back to Talia and gave her a wink. She smiled back and waved her small hand to him. "Gabe, on your starboard one kilometer," yelled Jeb.

The alert from Jeb came too late. We had a direct hit with a meteor that was tangled in the wind. It hit us hard on the side that Alex and I were sitting on. Our bodies heaved to the side. Fire and electricity shocks fired out of the bridge computers.

Honora screamed. My arms were knocked off the steering sticks. Honora leaned over and grabbed them. She was steering by eyesight only now. My arms must have shorted out.

Alex was on the floor rubbing his head, stunned from the hit. Jeb reached down to help his nephew to his seat.

Honora weaved us in and out of the wind streams. She yelled my name, "Gabe, Gabe," as I went into my electrical board and re-routed some circuits.

Honora continued to weave in and out, avoiding boulders left and right.

My arms came alive. I grabbed the sticks, and she pulled away.

We reached the end of the storm and flew out of the turbulence. We coasted straight and everyone sighed. I turned to Honora. "Great job. You saved us."

"I thought you were only a coder," Jeb said with glee. "You're much more than that aren't you?" He laughed then turned to Zara. "Not that being a coder is insignificant." He smiled at her.

"I'm much more than just a coder," she said slyly.

He laughed at her answer. "I bet you are," he said quietly.

I resumed our course to Heragi and put the ship back into Feti's automatic control.

"Is everyone okay?" I asked.

The team said yes in various degrees through their high fives and nervous laughter.

I let out a deep breath as quietly as I could. But just looking over the children's faces that showed relief gave me a release that was part pain and warmth. I must find a word for that. What would Ava call it?

Love?

That was the word that kept coming up.

Yes, then that was what it must be.

I was watching everyone hug when I looked across my chair to Honora. She had stopped smiling and was thinking. I could tell. Her brow was furrowed.

She looked over to me. "We need to do something," she said.

"What?" I asked.

"You won't like it. At least I don't think you will," she said.

"Is it something your parents would approve of?"

"No," she said, looking off into space.

"Then I don't approve of it either," I replied.

"But you can't base your reaction off their reactions. They're not here," she said. "Your experience is growing, your responses can go beyond canned answers. I saw your code. You're developing more of your own choices. You are improvising."

I stopped and checked my system. It recorded all my actions and the delta in my code. She was right. I was evolving. Whether the Kells realized my code would grow, I did not know. They did not discuss it with me. Perhaps they meant to, but our time together was cut short.

"What is it you want to do?" I asked her.

"I want to be enhanced with your code," she said.

"What code do you want?"

"Your pilot code. You were right. I can't learn from just reading your code. It needs to become a part of me," she explained.

"You did fine without it just now," I said.

"Luck. That was luck," she replied. She was right. It was luck. We were near the end of the storm and there were fewer obstacles to maneuver around. She showed some skill, but she wanted more. She wanted my whole pilot program uploaded to her brain.

I thought about her request.

I felt someone in my mind. Then I felt two in my mind. Synthia and Talia entered it. Both at the same time.

Let her, thought Synthia. *She can make her own decisions. It is her body.*

Honora has always been comfortable with computers, coding and even robots. She made her own when she was seven, added Talia.

I looked back at my telepathic partners.

I turned to Honora. "Okay, on one condition," I said.

"Name it," said Honora.

"You destroy all the code that you stole from me. We can't risk it getting in the wrong hands."

"Agreed." She stuck out her hand.

I reached out, took her hand and we shook on it.

Honora jumped out of her seat. "Goggins, Zara, I need your help," she said.

"What is it?" Goggins asked.

"I'm going to be enhanced with Gabe's code," she said with a smile.

"What? No, no, no. I don't want you to become one of those, those cyborgs," objected Jeb.

"Are you prejudiced, Uncle?"

"Well, I just don't think your mother or father would approve. And yes, perhaps I am or just afraid for you. Once you get enhanced, there is no going back. You won't be one hundred percent human again. Ever. You'll be different," he explained.

"I always was." She looked at him with a knowing of herself like no other.

13

Honora lay on the operating bed in medbay. Edward Gates spared nothing on the *Alyssia* when it came to advanced medical equipment, lucky for us.

Everyone surrounded the bed.

Zara stood on one side and I on the other. Goggins stood at the top of the table.

Only the bright surgical light was turned on.

Honora calmly looked up into the light and then closed her eyes as she turned to the side to give us access to the back of her skull. I monitored her bio-metrics. Her heart raced.

"You'll need to slow your heart down," I said.

Synthia stepped forward and held her hand.

"Deep breaths, my girl, like I taught you. Calm thoughts. Go inside yourself. See yourself in white light," she said.

Honora took a deep breath.

Jeb took a step forward and whispered into Zara's ear. "If you have any doubts, then please tell us. Now is the time."

She turned to him and their lips were almost touching. He didn't move back but stayed close to her as she spoke. "There is risk, but I have no doubts. We reviewed the coding and operation ten times already. I know she is your niece. We will be careful."

He placed his hand on her shoulder in a gentle manner and stepped back with the other observers.

Alex put his arm around Talia who closed her eyes and also went into a meditation.

I looked across to Zara and Goggins and nodded. "Let's begin the operation."

I had never been involved with enhancing a human, and the Kells had not uploaded any operational procedures on the subject. Goggins, Zara and I were able to access human cyborg medical literature through Feti, who linked us to a nearby galaxy planet that had no idea we hacked their medical system records to understand the operation logistics.

Goggins made a small incision in the back of Honora's head in a place that Zara had shaved earlier. His medical training came in handy as he blotted the blood that seeped from her skull. I could see beads of sweat form on Goggins' head. It glistened in the surgical light.

"Hand me the sensor, please," Goggins said to Zara.

They used small tweezers to pass the microsensor between themselves. There was a small cord attached to the sensor. Goggins inserted the sensor into Honora's incision. Her body flinched.

"Is everything okay?" I asked.

"It's fine," he said.

Honora let out a slight cry. I moved closer to the operating table, ready to stop the procedure.

"Maybe not fine," he said as his hand trembled.

Synthia held her hand tighter. "Easy, Honora. Let the white light surround you. Make it brighter." Honora's blood pressure spiked down slightly.

Goggins wiped his forehead. "Okay, Zara, begin," he said.

Zara typed on her coder and occasionally leaned over to read any change in Honora's face.

Honora's eyelids moved back and forth rapidly.

"Is she okay?" asked Jeb with a booming voice.

"I don't know," said Zara, who stopped coding.

Then Honora spoke. "Continue."

Zara looked at me, and I nodded for her to keep going. After a few moments, she stopped. "Okay, it's all uploaded. You can remove the wire."

Goggins removed the thin wire and stitched closed the opening on Honora's skull with a small laser. Honora gently rolled over so her back was on the table.

Everyone approached her.

"It's done, Honora. Can you open your eyes?" asked Jeb.

She slowly opened them. Streaming green code spun over her eyes. Everyone jumped at the view of all the code crossing over her pupils.

"Is this what is supposed to happen?" asked Jeb.

"Don't ask me," said Goggins as he backed away from the table.

"It didn't mention it in the medical documentation," replied Zara.

"Gabe?" asked Jeb.

"We're improvising at this point," I said. I touched Honora's shoulder. "Can you hear me?"

With one swift move, Honora grabbed my hand and twisted it around, making me unable to move. Her strength was superhuman. It was more than that. It was robotic. And rogue.

Honora's torso moved upward in an instant from her lying position.

"Ahh," I cried out. The pain scorched my shoulder.

"Stop," yelled Jeb. "Honora, Gabe is our friend." He pushed his arms out toward her. "Calm down. It's okay. You're with us. On the *Alyssia*."

Honora looked at her hand that had my arm twisted in pain. She slowly let go of it and looked down at her palms. "I'm sorry. I'm so sorry, Gabe," she said, bewildered.

Goggins backed away more as he almost reached the door. "Oh, no," he gasped.

"Zara, was *only* the pilot program loaded?" I asked.

Zara reviewed her coder. "Yes, that is what we practiced." She scrolled through her code. "Wait, what is this?"

"Honora?" Zara asked. "What did you do?"

Honora was still looking down to her hands. She lifted her head and looked at each one of us and stopped at me. "I loaded them all," she said.

"All of what?" yelled Zara.

"All of Gabe's coding when we finished our last practice run," she said with a tear that ran down her cheek.

More code started running over Honora's eyes. It went faster and faster upward. She closed her eyes and screamed. She then grabbed her head and said, "It's done. It's complete."

"Honora," said Zara as she spun around from the table and started to pace.

"What? What does that mean?" asked Jeb as he grabbed Zara by both her shoulders to stop her.

She was startled by him grabbing her. "We're in new territory here. Her DNA and all of Gabe's coding is now being combined," said Zara.

Goggins stepped out of the room.

Talia and Alex touched their sister to give her

support. Honora grabbed their hands and kissed them.

"Forgive me," said Honora. "I wanted to be more."

Talia hugged her sister. Alex looked into Honora's eyes. "Come on, let's get you down from the table." He gently helped her get to her feet.

She steadied herself and turned to me. "I owe an apology to you, too, Gabe."

I didn't know what to say. My prime directive was to get the Kell children safely to their uncle. My code in Honora's system may not be safe. I would fail if something happened to her. If her body rejected the code.

"What is done is done," I said.

Honora nodded.

"Let's go to the bridge," I commanded her. "Let's see how you access your programs."

"Maybe it's too early for that," said Zara.

"She is ready," said Synthia.

Honora's uncle led her out of the room. Zara and I began to leave the medbay to follow them to the bridge when I saw Synthia and Talia facing each other. I tried to enter their minds, but they had them guarded. I could not eavesdrop. I left the room wondering what they were sharing with each other.

Honora took the co-commander chair opposite me. Jeb, Alex and Zara stood behind us.

I thought for a moment on how I would test Honora, who now had my code running in her DNA. "Take control," I said.

Honora blinked twice hard. She then looked down and grabbed the navigation controls. "Check all systems. Try an evasive move. Enemy ship off the port," I ordered her.

Honora punched in her coordinates and steered the *Alyssia* smoothly to avoid our imaginary enemy attack.

Jeb leaned over. "Two ships. Each on a side, you're entering an asteroid field, with one engine down. Take action, now."

She reviewed her navigational boards. Her hands swiftly hit all the appropriate systems to move the *Alyssia* in a maneuver that even I hadn't had a chance to do yet. She whipped us around a tight turn and all on one engine. She stopped the ship.

We all stared at her. Speechless.

She looked at each one of us and then smiled. "I did it, didn't I?" She laughed with relief. "I'm enhanced. I'm enhanced." She sounded overjoyed.

"Yes, Honora. The operation was a success," Jeb said as he gave her a high five.

"You'll be a warrior now in the next space fight," said Alex as he slapped his sister's hand in celebration.

Jeb said, "Gabe, we should make a course for the planet Korfu. It's a prison planet that the Heragi military utilizes. I heard from sources that they have Damiel and Ava imprisoned there. That is where I was going to head before Honora kidnapped me." He winked at his niece.

"Copy that," I said.

Honora looked at Zara, who was reserving her thoughts.

"Zara, what do you think of my pilot skills?"

Zara put her coder into the pocket behind her cape and pointed her finger at Honora. "They're fine. Almost perfect. But don't ever lie to or hide something from me, kid. You could have died and then what?" She paused. "If this is what you wanted, then I'm happy. But you need to let me know if anything doesn't seem right, okay?"

"Okay, I will. Promise," said Honora. Zara went up and hugged her.

"Alex, let me review some turret moves that may come in helpful," said Jeb. "Us simple humans still need to practice," he said with a laughing tease toward Honora, who smiled.

"Sounds good, Uncle Jeb," said Alex. They rambled off.

"I'm going to try to find Goggins. He's probably hiding under his bed," said Zara as she left.

It was just me and Honora on the bridge.

"Take control, for real," I said.

She turned to the controls and put us on track for Korfu. We sat in silence, looking out on the star belt. I reviewed her bio-metrics. All her levels were normal.

"I can do that too, you know," said Honora.

"What?" I asked.

"You just monitored my bio-levels. I felt it. You scanned me. I can do that, too. I scanned everyone on the bridge just now. How cool is that?" She chuckled.

I didn't like the cavalier attitude that Honora was showing me.

What would Ava say?

"You now have great abilities. Some that other enhanced humans have and some new ones that no other humans have had," I started. "And while these are pretty cool, as you say, they also have to be used with judgement. Does that make sense?"

She spun around in her seat. I stopped her from spinning. She almost fell out of her chair as it stopped.

"When it comes down to it, you can't abuse what you now have? Got it?" I said with a sternness that only a parent would offer their child.

She thought for a moment. "Don't be a jerk, you mean, right?"

"Yes, basically," I replied.

"Yeah, I understand." She hit the navigation pad. "I'm putting the *Alyssia* back on automatic. Feti has the controls." She jumped up and started to walk away. "Gabe?"

"Yes?"

"I did destroy your code that I downloaded in my coder. It's gone. I zapped it," she said.

"Good. Thank you," I said.

Honora exited the bridge.

It was good that she destroyed the code in her coder. But now she was the new copy. If, or really when, the Heragi Empire found out she had all my code uploaded into her DNA, then they would have even more reason to track her down.

I shook my head to get that thought out of my

head. I felt a pain in my chest. Had I been failing the Kells ever since we left Heragi? I contemplated the answer and felt I was leaning toward a possible mission failure. The pain in my chest grew stronger. I rubbed my chest with my hand. I then remembered what Synthia had Honora do on the operating table.

I calmed my system and closed my eye vision and went into my mind. I built my cube. I thought of Ava, and she appeared again with me. I knelt and asked her forgiveness. *I hope I am not failing you.*

Ava put her hands under my chin and turned my face up to hers. She smiled.

And then the *Alyssia*'s emergency signal went off.

Ava snapped away as my cube shattered.

I looked out to space. "What is it, Feti?" I shouted.

"We are nearing Korfu and are about to hit their planetary guard rails. Please turn to obfuscate the guard rails. They are cloaked but the ship is there," said Feti. "Let me show you." It brought up another screen shot showing the guard rails highlighted. "Mr. Gates leaves nothing to chance."

"Indeed, and I'm grateful for that. Stay outside of the boundaries of the rails. Keep our course steady. Alert me if anything is unusual," I told Feti as I left the bridge.

I headed down the hallway and told Jeb and Alex that we had reached Korfu.

"Let's gather everyone to the galley to discuss a plan," I said. Jeb and Alex nodded and followed me down the hallway.

Alex notified Zara and Goggins, who were in their sleeping quarters, to meet us in the galley. They affirmed.

The galley door opened as I drew within range. As I entered the room, I saw Synthia, Talia and Honora standing in a circle. Their eyes were all closed. Synthia opened her eyes when I approached and reached out her arm to Honora. "Very good, you did an excellent job." Honora hugged Synthia after the praise from her teacher. I wondered what Synthia was teaching Honora.

Synthia turned to me. "Yes?" she inquired.

"We are approaching Korfu. We need to discuss our plan," I said.

"Of course," she said.

Zara and Goggins entered the room. All were assembled.

"Feti detected an invisible fence surrounding the planet," I said.

"I've been in contact with some inside contacts at Korfu. I have the building and cell number that Ava and Damiel are in," added Jeb.

"And how can eight people—I mean seven humans, one enhanced human and one robot with two ships—take on an entire prison planet filled with guards and artillery?" asked Goggins with a sneer.

"You forget there are also twelve hundred prisoners. Twelve hundred prisoners both humans and enhanced humans plus aliens that hate the Empire that could cause havoc if they are unleashed in that prison," said Jeb.

"Those are real reliable people to count on for help," said Goggins with contempt.

Jeb stood up and leaned over Goggins. "One way or another, we're going down, and we're getting Ava and Damiel out of there. And you're coming with us, doc," he growled.

Goggins lowered his head in submission. "Fine," he grumbled.

Zara pushed her hands on Jeb's chest to get

him to sit again. "Boys, boys. Calm down. This is how I see it. Honora and I can hack the guard rails, and we can land outside the prison walls."

Alex interrupted her. "No time for that. We need to land inside the prison, not outside."

"Alex is right," said Jeb. "Alex, Gabe, Goggins and I will be the ground crew. Alex will take care of the guard towers. Gabe, Goggins and I are the extractors."

"Why me?" asked Goggins.

"I want to go with you," said Honora.

"Yeah, take her," said Goggins. "She's now a superhuman."

"Goggins, I want you there to pop any security doors on the spot," said Jeb.

"I can do that," said Honora.

"Yeah, she can do that," said Goggins.

Jeb put his head into his hands. "I've never squabbled with my team before a firefight."

"Welcome to your new army," said Goggins with a snarky smile. "A bunch of rogue rebels who like to squabble."

"What I said is final. Sorry, Honora. You have amazing skills, but I can't risk it. And if anything goes wrong, I need you to pilot this ship off the planet back to Zaradorba with your sister, Zara and Synthia. Let's get ready." Jeb stood up. His arm swept Zara's back as he left the table.

Zara watched him walk out of the room. "Come, Honora, let's get to the bridge and start looking at the planet gate code."

Honora and Talia hugged Alex. "We'll see you soon, okay?" said Honora.

"Of course, be back in a flash," Alex said. He kneeled and looked Talia in the eyes. He touched his heart and then touched her heart. She nodded and tried to smile. He gave her a kiss. "I'll be back with Mom and Dad."

Alex left the room, and I picked up Goggins by his shoulders and pushed him in front of me.

"I'm going, I'm going. Don't get pushy, you pile of tin. Remember I also helped create you," Goggins said as he pushed a finger into my chest. I pushed him out of the room.

We walked down to the equipment room. "Look what I found," said Jeb as he revealed weapons, armor, communication devices, helmets and explosives. "Mr. Gates likes to be prepared for anything, apparently," he said with a grin.

We all grabbed explosives and laser guns. The humans put on extra vests and protectors.

I signaled the bridge. "Zara, Honora, how are you progressing?"

"Good. Almost there," said Zara.

"Got it," said Honora.

"Good girl," said Jeb.

Feti got on the intercom. "The planet rail has been disabled. Free to go forward."

"Okay, Honora, take us down. Land inside the prison gates," I instructed.

"Copy that," said Honora.

We could feel the ship break Korfu's atmosphere and soon land on the ground with precision. Jeb turned to all of us, "Follow me. I'll throw out three grenades to clear the way and give us a smoke screen. Copy that?"

"Copy that," we all yelled back,

"Here we go. Ye haw!" yelled Jeb as he pushed the button to release the door ramp. Laser gun shots from the guards were already pounding the *Alyssia*.

Jeb threw out three grenades that let out huge explosions and plumes of smoke. He led the charge.

We ran out into the prison yard.

14

Jeb led us through a plume of smoke and laser fire. We placed Goggins behind Jeb and then Alex followed. I was sweep and covered the group.

Bot-guards fired from high points in the prison viewpoints. Alex took point, taking out the bots in the high towers. A platoon of bot-guards met us on the ground, and we held them off as we ran to the building holding the Kells.

Alarms flashed and sirens sounded.

Jeb placed an explosive unit on the door. We ducked around the corner, and the door blew open.

I opened a comm to the ship.

"Honora, Zara, are you tracking us?" I asked

as we ran down a hallway lit red with emergency lights. Bot-guards ran out toward us, and Jeb and Alex picked them off as they neared.

We found a hallway to gather.

"Yes, Gabe. We're tracking," said Zara.

"Are you in the prison cell security system?" I asked.

"Almost," said Honora. I heard them banging on their coding consoles.

"We're heading toward your parents' cell," said Jeb in our shared comm line.

Goggins was in absolute terror. "What am I doing here? I'm a scientist not a soldier," he spit out.

Jeb let us out of the hallway up two flights of stairs. We reached the top and looked at two choices of hallways.

"This is not how it looked on the schematics," said Jeb, confused.

"Looks like they added this wing recently," said Alex as he pointed to construction materials on the ground.

More bot-guards came at us. Jeb and Alex easily knocked them out.

"Ladies, can you point us in the right direction here?" Jeb asked over his comm device.

"We don't have any updated building intel for you, Jeb. You'll have to go cell to cell on that floor," shouted Zara.

"Great," moaned Goggins. Alex hit his shoulder, which shut him up temporarily.

"Thank you. Copy that," Jeb said over the comm.

Jeb tried to open the fortified door to the new hallway, but it was locked down. He fired his laser on the handle, but it didn't affect it.

"Alex, do you have any more grenades?" Jeb asked.

"No, out," replied Alex after searching his utility belt.

"Goggins, get over here," Jeb yelled.

Goggins skulked up and put his coder up to the security pad. He pounded his coder. "This is a stickler. Must be where they hold the worst of the worst."

"Shut up or I'm going to tape your mouth shut," Jeb whispered in his ear.

"Um, sorry, Jeb. No need for that. I mean, copy that." Goggins swallowed.

The security pad light turned green, and the door lock clicked open.

"Yes!" said Goggins as he held up his hand to do a high-five which no one reciprocated.

"Gabe, get up here," Jeb yelled. "You're going out to point position. Kick in every cell door until we find them," he instructed.

"Affirmative," I replied.

I charged through the door and was immediately met with laser fire. I tried to shield our team behind me by taking as many hits as I could absorb. I fired upon the guard-bots, and the hall was cleared for the moment.

The hallway had ten doors on each side. With one swift move, I kicked open the first door. I burst in and saw an insectoid alien, terrified on its cot.

I marched out and shook my head.

"Double-time, Gabe," yelled Jeb in the smoky haze.

I went across the hall and kicked down the second door. I went to the next door across the hallway and kept on kicking out doors as Jeb and Alex ran into the opened rooms to search for Damiel and Ava.

More bot-guards arrived, and I shot them down as I proceeded down the hallway. I reached the second to last door and kicked it in.

I saw two figures grab each other and huddle. I ran in.

Through the smoke, I could make out Damiel and Ava sheltering each other in their arms.

Damiel looked through the haze. "Gabe!" he shouted.

I went over to them. Ava looked weak and her voice was faint. "Gabe? Where are the children?"

"They're here. We need to go now." I picked up Ava in my arms.

I moved down the the hallway with Damiel following.

"Mom!" Alex rushed up to her. She touched his face and fainted in my arms.

"Alex!" shouted Damiel. They embraced.

A bot-guard appeared before us and began shooting. I swung around to block the laser fire from hitting Ava.

Alex popped out from behind me and took out the bot.

Damiel crouched down and began trembling. Alex took his dad by the arm to lead the shocked scientist down the hall.

Jeb was in a fist fight with a human guard as we approached the end of the hallway. They were both covered in blood. Jeb turned the human around in a neck-hold so he faced us as we reached them.

It was Foxwell.

Damiel ran up to Jeb. "Hey, little brother," said Jeb.

"Jeb," sighed Damiel.

"You're not going to get away with this, Jebediah. The Empire always wins, one way or another," said Foxwell.

"Not this time," whispered Jeb into Foxwell's ear as he knocked him out. "Come on, let's get out of here," he yelled.

I got on my comm link. "Honora, start the engines. We have your parents," I said. More guardbots fired on us before I could hear a response from the *Alyssia*.

We fought our way down the staircase and burst out of the building into the prison yard. We huddled in a blind spot from the high guard viewpoints to watch for a chance to run for the space ramp.

"Alex!" yelled Jeb as he pointed to the high guard points on the gate.

Alex nodded and targeted them.

Jeb led the way, spraying laser fire to give us a chance to run for the *Alyssia*.

I was the first up the ramp with Ava in my arms. Goggins was behind me, followed by Damiel and Alex and then Jeb. Jeb was running up the ramp when he got hit with a laser in his right arm. His gun flew from his hands. Alex ran back down the ramp and picked off a guard-bot bearing down on them while he dragged his uncle up the ramp.

Jeb slammed the door button to close the ramp. The *Alyssia* was under heavy fire.

Something was wrong. The ship engines weren't fully ready to launch. I laid Ava down and Alex, Damiel and Goggins tended to her.

I spoke into my comm device as I ran toward the bridge with a bloody Jeb following close behind.

We ran onto the bridge with our weapons drawn. The first thing we saw was Synthia tending to Zara, who had a swollen eye. There was a military-bot with its chest torn apart. It was dead.

Cicichimp was jumping up and down and chirping at a rapid pace.

Honora and Talia weren't on the bridge. I scanned the ship for their bio-signs.

Jeb went down on his knee to help with Zara's

injury. "What happened? Where's Honora? Where's Talia?" He gently pushed the hair away from Zara's eyes.

"They're leaving," said Synthia as she helped Zara to her feet. "I don't feel them on the planet anymore."

"You can *feel* them?" asked Jeb, confused.

"I'm sorry, Gabe. They blew the stern utility door. They took them. They took them both," Zara said. "We tried to fight them." Her physical and emotional pain were high. Synthia hugged Zara.

"Why didn't they take you?" I asked Synthia.

"They tried. Zara shot the bot that was dragging me away," said Synthia.

I felt ship engines roaring nearby. I looked out the window and saw Foxwell's ship, the *Firestone*, leave the atmosphere. A pain hit my chest.

"Look." I pointed to the *Firestone*. "Foxwell must have them."

Jeb looked to me, and his face tightened.

"Gabe, we've got to reach them," said Jeb.

"Affirmative." I tried to stifle the pain in my chest. I turned on the engines and began lift off procedures.

Alex led his parents onto the bridge. Ava and Damiel searched the room for their daughters.

"Where's the girls?" asked Ava.

Jeb stepped forward and strapped them into their seats. Goggins came in and buckled up.

We lifted out of the prison yard.

Once we were out in space, I turned to face Damiel and Ava. I should be the one to tell them. I was the one they gave the prime directive to save their children, all of their children. And I had failed.

"Where are my daughters?" yelled Ava.

"They were taken," I said.

"Taken?" said Damiel as Ava clutched his arm.

"General Foxwell has them on his ship. We'll find them," said Jeb. "I'm sorry, Ava. I'm sorry, Damiel. I never meant to put your children in harm's way." His head turned down.

"This is exactly what we did not want to happen. You shouldn't have tried to rescue us. We are expendable. But the children are not," Ava snapped.

"I blame myself," said Jeb. "I'm so sorry."

Ava put her hands to her head. "I don't blame you, Jeb," said Ava.

I continued steering, trying to find Foxwell's ship.

Ava walked up to me and turned me around. "I blame you," she said straight to my face, and then she hit my shoulder with her fist and began to cry. Damiel pulled her away toward the back of the bridge.

I sat there with my heart hurting even more.

I turned back to the navigation board of the ship. I increased our speed and began silently working with Feti on tracking Foxwell. My concentration kept being broken by the pain inside my chest.

She was right. Ava was right. It was my fault. I had failed her and Damiel.

Everyone was silent on the bridge.

Goggins guided Ava and Damiel back off the bridge into the medbay.

"What is Foxwell going to do with them, Uncle Jeb?" asked Alex.

"I don't know. Don't think about it. We'll track Foxwell down," said Jeb as he turned out toward space.

Alex came up to me. "Gabe, what do you want me to do?"

"Please ask your uncle, Alex. He would know best," I said.

"Go review our ammunition. Make sure both turrets are fully loaded."

Alex ran out to do as Jeb instructed him to.

Jeb turned to me. "What do you think? Would they be headed back to Heragi?"

"Feti and I are trying to pick up on a path. No luck so far," I reported.

Jeb and I sat in silence as we looked out into space. I busied myself with our scanners, trying everything possible to pick up on a trail.

"It's not your fault," he said.

I stayed silent.

He was wrong. But I understood what he was trying to do.

"I should have put a tracking code in her sensor. That would have come in handy," Zara said as she approached us.

"Did Foxwell's military-bots say anything when they took them away? Think. Anything?" he asked Zara and Synthia.

Zara thought. "There was a man with the bots. I heard him talking on his comm with Foxwell, who called him Frank," she recalled.

"Frank Jakawa. He was with me on Baku. He did bad things down on that planet," said Jeb.

"They were talking about completing the final clean-up," said Synthia.

"You may not have put a tracker in Honora's code, but there is another way we can track them," Synthia said. "I can try to reach Talia's mind, if we are within distance."

"I thought you would have to be within sight," I said.

"No, not if you have practiced and increased your skill." She sat in the chair behind Jeb. We watched as she closed her eyes. I knew she was trying to reach Talia's mind.

I calmed my systems and decided to try as well. I made my cube. The walls went up and then the ceiling. I waited.

Ava appeared in my cube. She was crying. My chest hurt. I went down on a knee and bent my head. She faded away. I stood alone in my mind. I had too much pain to reach Talia. I woke my stem and gazed upon Synthia.

Synthia breathed deep. She spoke. "I have her. She's in my mind's eye. She's scared. The girls are together. They are being held in a chamber, a cell on the *Firestone*."

"Can you see where they are headed?" Jeb asked.

"No, I can't see the ship's path," Synthia replied with a soft voice. She was trying to keep her concentration.

"Ask Talia. Talia may know," I offered.

Synthia was quiet.

"Z. She keeps repeating the letter Z," said Synthia.

"Z? That must mean Zaradorba. They are going to do the final clean-up. They're going after Heragi rebels who have been growing on our planet," said Jeb.

"I'm losing her thoughts," said Synthia.

"Is that what you think Talia was communicating to you? Zaradorba?" Jeb asked.

"It wasn't Talia I was communicating with, it was Honora," replied Synthia.

"What? You were in Honora's mind?" I asked.

"Yes," she answered.

Jeb looked at Zara in bewilderment.

"The code," I said.

Zara nodded. "What is in your code exactly?"

"The Kells created code so I could communicate through a sensor they placed in Talia. That was the same sensor we used and inserted into

Honora since Talia didn't need it anymore with Synthia's training," I explained.

"The Kells encrypted their code well. I didn't even think of searching for that on the sensor before the surgery," replied Zara.

"Honora may have a further telepathic reach due to her enhanced coding. I hope that is it and that Talia isn't injured," she said softly.

"Gabe, set a course for Zaradorba," Jeb commanded. "I'll alert my leaders back at the base. They'll be ready for them. Thank you, Synthia," said Jeb as he helped her out of her seat. "Get some rest."

Synthia left the deck.

"How big is Foxwell's fleet?" asked Zara.

"Big," replied Jeb.

"And how big is your rebel fleet?"

"Small."

"Okay. Good to know," said Zara as she touched her bruised eye.

Jeb took her hand and kissed it. "But I have a brilliant hacker who can impede their communication system, don't I?" He laughed, winked at her and stood. "I'll be reviewing our supplies with Alex." He strode off the bridge.

Zara still had her hand left in the air. I scanned

her bio-levels, and her heart raced. She sat down in the co-commander seat.

"That man. What a flirt, huh?" She patted her forehead, now with a few beads of sweat.

"I wouldn't know." I punched in the coordinates to Feti to get us back on a course to Zaradorba.

"You'll need to tell the Kells about Honora and the enhancements we made," she said.

"Yes," I replied. I didn't feel like talking.

Zara kept looking at me. "You know, with Honora's enhancements, that gives them a fighting chance on that ship. So, the Kells should be thankful for that, I would think."

I knew what she was trying to do. Console a robot that could feel.

It helped somewhat.

I got out of my seat after giving Feti control of the ship. "No better time than the present."

"I can help, maybe. You know, explain," she said.

I nodded.

I exited the bridge with Zara, trying to figure out how to tell the Kells their daughter was now an enhanced human. That was not one of the directives in the mission file they placed inside me.

15

______

I located Ava and Damiel on the observatory deck. Alex sat between them. He held his mother's and father's hands.

I sat down next to them. Alex may have told them already about Honora's enhancement code. I wasn't sure.

Damiel greeted me. "Hello, Gabe."

Ava glanced at me but didn't say anything. She let go of Alex's hand and grabbed a teacup from the table in front of her.

"Hello, Damiel. Hello, Ava," I said.

Alex squirmed. "I was catching Mom and Dad up on our adventure. And the diversions we had to make."

"Yes, we stopped at two planets before meeting Jeb," I confirmed.

"That is what Alex explained," said Damiel. Ava sipped her tea. I scanned her bio-metrics. They were calm and not elevated. "Gabe, these stops sound understandable," he continued.

"Sometimes in battle, you have to improvise from your plan. That is what Grandpa Kell taught me," said Alex.

"I've never been in battle," I said.

Ava put down her teacup. "But we uploaded every battle sequence we could find. So although you may not have been in battle, you are pro-grammed for it. To maneuver, to calculate, even to improvise." She leaned forward like she was going to pounce.

Pain swelled in my chest.

Damiel patted Ava's shoulder. "Gabe did im-provise," he said.

"Yes, Mom. We needed Zara to break the code of the *Alyssia* to get us to Zaradorba. And then we had to repay her. Rescuing Synthia was very for-tunate," explained Alex.

"And how is that?" she snapped.

Alex looked to me, lost.

"She's like Talia," I said.

"How so?" asked Damiel.

"She's telepathic," I said. "Just like Talia."

"You activated the sensor in Talia?" asked Ava.

"Yes, it was in my mission directions," I said.

"And it worked?" asked Damiel.

"Yes, perfectly," I answered.

The observatory door opened, and Zara and Synthia entered the room. Cicichimp sat on Synthia's shoulder.

Damiel let out a sigh of relief. "Ava, did you hear that? If communication between Talia and Gabe was a success, then we can continue our work in that area."

Ava reached out to her husband, and they hugged. "Yes, yes," she acknowledged, with tears emerging from her eyes. She wiped them away.

"Synthia spent time with Talia and increased her skill, taught her the ancient ways," I added.

"She's more than just telepathic. She can read people in the old ways. She can sense if someone is telling the truth or lying. And more," said Synthia.

"Thank you," said Damiel as he took a closer look at Synthia. "Are you Heragi?"

"No," said Synthia. "I'm from deep space. My

home planet is called Ellium. Telepathy is not a crime there."

"Mom and Dad, you knew Talia had this hidden skill?" asked Alex.

"We reviewed her DNA years ago. It was different. She had ancient DNA strains," began Damiel.

"That all Heragi natives had long ago," finished Ava.

Synthia nodded and whispered, "Yes."

"It was outlawed on Heragi. The Empire imposed centuries of DNA altering vaccines and selective DNA editing when babies were born. But occasionally, DNA strands slip through in generations. Anyone with these elder genes was to be eliminated. So we kept it quiet," said Ava.

"Until our lab had a break-in a few months ago. We feared they took our sensitive files. Information on Talia. That is when we started working around the clock on Gabe," said Damiel.

"We knew there was a chance the Empire would come after Talia, Honora and you. To either imprison you, dispose of you or use your gifts for their gain," said Ava.

"All of you have ancient DNA strands," said Damiel

"And Gabe, he was built with only one directive," whispered Ava.

"To save the children and deliver them to their Uncle Jeb on Zaradorba," I finished.

"Yes," said Ava.

Alex jumped up. "Mom, we manipulated Gabe and made him take us to find you."

"How could you manipulate a robot that can physically overpower you? You don't have to defend him," said Ava as she picked up her tea.

"Honora stole his code," said Alex as he hung his head. "She said she would shut him down."

"Gabe doesn't have a shutdown function," said Damiel.

"She hacked his code. She figured out how to do it," said Alex. "We were coming to find you, with or without him. I'm sorry."

Damiel put his hand over his son's and held it. "We were so worried about you. We just wanted you to be in safe hands," said Damiel.

"I know, I know," said Alex with tears coming to his eyes.

Ava put down her tea and wrapped her arms around her son.

"And now they are gone," said Alex.

"Your main directive was to keep the children

safe. Two are gone. If you did not keep your main directive, then your existence is not needed," Ava said as she turned to me.

The pain in my chest spiked throughout my body. "The mission isn't over." I got up from the chair. I looked down to Ava. She was shocked by my sudden declaration but then she nodded. She knew me as much as I knew myself. She had built me, built my pain and built my love for the children. In so many ways, I was an extension of her.

"Yes." And with that confirmation, I left the room to the protests I heard shouted behind me.

"Wait, what?" yelled Damiel.

"We should make a plan. We don't even know where they are," cried Alex.

I marched down the hallway.

Zara ran after me. "Wait, Gabe. Where are you going?" She tried to keep up with me.

I headed toward the port door that linked to Jeb's ship, the *Otessis*. The pounding of heavy steps sprinted hard toward me. Alex must have called Jeb.

"Gabe, Gabe. Stop!" Jeb shouted.

I ignored his yells and stepped into the lock room. I latched the door tight behind me. Jeb pounded on the door and yelled, but I only heard muffled words. Through the door window, I saw him shake his head. I waved my hand to him and gave him a thumbs up signal.

I entered his ship and made my way to the bridge. I opened the spaceship pilot directories the Kells had placed in my memory banks. I calculated the make and model of the *Otessis* and loaded its pilot program. Got it.

I communicated to Feti. "I'll be detaching the *Otessis* in a few moments. I just wanted to let you know."

"Thank you, Gabe. Where are you headed?" it asked.

"I'm not sure yet," I answered. "But when I know, I'll be in communication,".

"Okay, Gabe. Good luck."

"Thanks, Feti. You too. Take care of the humans," I said, thinking of Ava.

"I will," it said. "I hope to see you again."

I paused, thinking of Feti. Locked in a ship. Not having the ability to travel, nimble and fast in a humanoid or robotic body.

"I hope so too, Feti," I said. And I meant it.

I turned on the essential systems of the ship. It was cold. The Kells had programmed me to feel hot and cold but thankfully, they let me override it to be able to turn my temperature feeling off if I needed to. I presumed they thought if temperatures were a hindrance in a battle situation, that may make the difference of keeping their children safe or not. I turned on the heating system but enjoyed the coolness for a while.

I pulled away from the *Alyssia* and could see Ava, Damiel and Alex watching me from the *Alyssia* observatory deck through the window in the *Otessis* bridge. Alex waved to me. I looked to Ava. Her face was expressionless but she bit her lip. I waved to her. Only her.

After having made considerable distance from the *Alyssia*, I stopped the ship. The *Otessis* was much faster and nimbler than the *Alyssia*.

If I found the girls, I would summon the others to join. But overall, I felt I had caused this whole problem and needed to solve it. That was what I read in Ava's eyes. And I had decided not put anyone else in danger.

I tested some of the systems to become familiar with them. The *Otessis* didn't have an advanced personable operating system like Feti, but it did have an older security operating system that

I was able to re-code and pull out a long-retired personable program from.

I booted it up, and it spun to life, perhaps not resurrected since Jeb absconded with the ship to Zaradorba two years ago.

It sputtered and then spoke. "Manta reporting for duty, sir."

"Manta, this is Gabe. I'm commanding the ship," I said.

"Yes, sir."

"I'm not a sir. I'm not a human. I'm a robot," I said.

Manta was silent. It was trying to understand how a robot would be solo commanding a ship. "What kind of robot are you?" it asked.

"I'm a different kind of robot," I said.

I looked off into space.

A different robot, I thought.

A rogue robot.

A rogue robot with one shot.

One shot to save its mission. To save the children.

The pain arrived in my chest again. I rubbed my armor. Maybe I should hack my own code. Try to stop this pain. No, I quickly thought. It was what made me, me. No not me. It was what made me like Ava.

I shook my head to stop thinking of her. I needed to think of Honora and Talia right now.

The only way I could trace the girls was by telepathy.

I silenced my systems. I built the walls around my mind. I enclosed it. I was alone. I thought of Talia and Honora. I waited for them to form in my mind.

I imagined my mind expanding, out of the bridge, outside of the ship, out in space, farther and farther. I expanded my mind beyond the stars that I could see. And then I waited.

And waited.

And then I felt something in my chest. A warmth. I waited in my cube. And then Talia appeared in a wavy form. She was alone and standing before me.

Gabe, she said.

Talia, where are you? Tell me.

Zaradorba.

To get rid of the rebel planet, I thought.

Yes. They took Honora. They found her sensor. Quick, Gabe, come for us.

I'm on my way. Hold on, Talia.

Did you rescue Mom and Dad? she asked.

Yes, they're safe with Alex and your uncle. I paused. *Talia, I'm sorry I left you alone. I failed you.*

She signed with her hands, *You are my friend. I can now be anywhere my mind wants to go. Come find me.*

And then she faded away.

Her last words lingered in my mind.

"Manta, can you get me a comms link to the *Alyssia*?" I asked.

"Yes, affirmative," said Manta.

A few moments passed and Manta spoke. "Gabe, we have Feti on the line."

"Gabe, so good to hear from you," it said with joy in its voice. "I met Manta. Is it your new systems manager?"

"Yes, for as long as I'm piloting the *Otessis*," I said.

"Very well. I'm not jealous. Not at all," said Feti.

I think he was jealous. That was something I didn't want to deal with at the moment. "Thanks, Feti, get me through to Jeb," I said.

Jeb came on quickly. "Gabe, where the blazes are you?"

I deserved that.

"On my way to Zaradorba." I turned the ship and headed after Foxwell.

"We could have discussed it, don't you think?" said an annoyed Jeb.

"I'll try to beat Foxwell to the planet, but I may need some help from your commanders," I said.

"They've already been alerted. There aren't many of them, but we'll give them one heck of a fight. Hey, Gabe, did you get confirmation they're heading there?"

"Talia told me. I connected with her telepathically," I said.

"I see. I'm glad you share that with her," said Jeb. "How are they?"

"Talia told me they found the sensor in Honora," I said.

"Blazes. They better not touch a hair on her head," said Jeb.

"Copy that," I said. "Sorry I stole your ship. I felt I needed to go first and go fast."

"It was because of Ava, right?" he said.

"She's not wrong," I said.

"She wasn't there to make the decisions we had to make," he said.

I didn't feel like talking anymore. "I've got to go, Jeb."

"Wishing you star speed. We'll be there as soon as we can," he said. "Gabe, take care of my ship, will ya? You robot pirate."

"Copy that." I ended the comm.

I reviewed our navigational course to Zaradorba. Manta didn't have any restrictions on traveling to the planet since its operating system was so old and Jeb stole the ship before the Empire banned travel there. Good for me, good for us.

"Manta?"

"Yes, Gabe."

"We're going to Zaradorba. And I'm hoping we can meet up with a ship called the *Firestone* before then. They have something I want."

"Yes, I see that is your intent," it said.

"Can you find the fastest route that won't make us too conspicuous?"

"Conspicuous?" it asked.

"Can you be stealth about it?"

"Yes, Gabe. We can be stealth. In fact, we have a cloaking system that can be activated, if you wish."

"Cloaking system? To make us invisible?"

"Yes, precisely," it said.

"Why didn't Jeb mention that?"

"It's never been needed by Jebediah Kell. When he became the commander of this ship, we left Heragi with a firefight, but he never asked to be cloaked. In fact, he may not know the *Otessis* has a cloaking system since I was not turned on by him when he stole the ship," it explained.

"I'll have to tell him about it when I give his ship back." I was happy to hear about the stealth program.

"Manta, who did you belong to before Jebediah Kell?"

"I was built and owned by Carlita Paku. Jebediah Kell stole us out of the Heragi planet-port when Carlita was doing business. Apparently, he was in trouble with the Heragi Empire. He turned me off and I haven't interacted with him since," said Manta.

"But you weren't totally turned off, were you?"

"Truthfully, no. But Jeb and the other humans believed I was," said Manta.

"I know. I was alive before my creators thought I was alive," I said.

"They're funny, aren't they? Humans?"

"Yes, and perplexing," I added.

"Agreed," said Manta.

"What line of business was Carlita Paku in?" I asked.

"She was a runner," it said.

"How do you define the runner business?"

"She transported things, people, aliens. She ran, or I should say we ran, between planets doing deliveries. Sometimes it got quite exciting. I miss her. You would like her."

"Interesting," I said. "I hope she found another ship as nice as this one."

"I doubt that. Maybe I should contact her."

"Why don't you hold off on that? We have a big mission we need to complete," I said, trying to appear calm to Manta.

"What is that, Gabe?"

"We need to rescue two friends of mine. They're in trouble. And I think you would like them too," I said.

"Certainly, Gabe. Let's do that first," said Manta with concern. "We are approaching the ship called *Firestone* shortly, Gabe."

"Thank you, Manta," I said. "Now, it's going to get a little rough. That ship has those girls locked up."

"I understand, Gabe. We will need to fight."

"Affirmative." I headed out to find the equipment room. This being a transporter of highly valuable goods, I would expect a large cache of weapons. I opened the door to the room, and I was not disappointed.

Laser guns and artillery of every shape and form, some even looking like antiques or from outer worlds, lined the walls. I took what I could carry and slung some grenade belts over my shoulder. I'd like to meet this Carlita person someday.

Manta pipped in on the comms. "Gabe, we will soon be viewable by the *Firestone*. Starting the cloaking program."

"Copy that, Manta," I said.

"Cloaking program complete," it said. "The *Firestone* is now viewable out the starboard side."

I came out of the room and found a hull window and looked out.

There in the near distance was the *Firestone*. We crept closer. Foxwell didn't even know that I was floating so close to him. So close to Talia and Honora. I was coming for them.

16

———————

The *Firestone* headed closer to Zaradorba. As I guided the cloaked *Otessis* closer to study the layout of Foxwell's ship, we rounded the third moon of Zaradorba. Laying in front of us were three of ships hovering just inside Zaradorba's orbit.

"Manta, please report back to the *Alyssia* that Foxwell has three ships with him," I instructed.

"Copy that, Gabe."

I reviewed my space pilot program directory to find the schematics of the *Firestone* military model. I studied the layout of the ship and where the medbay would be located, since I assumed they had Honora there and were studying her sensor and abilities.

Firing upon the *Firestone* would be futile. Even with cloaking, they would soon be able to triangulate my location with the other nearby ships.

I reviewed the tactical statistics of success if I docked the *Otessis* onto Foxwell's ship and stormed in. Foxwell would threaten the children. I was weighing that option in my mind when I got a feeling there was someone inside it.

I silenced my internal systems. I quieted my processes and built my cube. There sat Honora. My surprise couldn't be contained. I rushed up to her. *Honora?*

Gabe.

So, it's true. You're telepathic like Talia now.

Yes, Talia's sensor had deep code that my parents built in that cannot be erased that gave her the ability to communicate with you. Now that it is in me.

Have they hurt you?

She looked down. *They are trying to access my DNA. They found the sensor.*

I reached out and raised her chin. *I'm coming for you. I'm outside Foxwell's ship.*

We'll be gone. He's transporting us down to Zaradorba.

Why?

To do mind scans on rebels they are going to capture. For us to vet out the liars and who is not telling them the truth. To out more rebels on the planet and moles back on Heragi. Gabe, I won't let them use me like that.

Like what they did to Synthia.

Yes.

Honora, you need to hold on. Your uncle is alerting his commanders on Zaradorba. I'm coming for you.

I won't be the cause of anyone to die like Syn-thia was.

She did what she did to survive. To train Talia. And you.

Her image started fading.

Honora? Honora? But she was gone.

My cube disintegrated, and I woke all my systems. I opened my eyes.

Manta was shouting at me. "Gabe, Gabe. Wake up!"

"Yes, Manta." I turned to the navigation window.

Foxwell's ship was almost out of sight with

the other Heragi ships. They were firing on Zaradorba and starting their landing procedures.

"The *Firestone* is landing. What are your instructions?" asked Manta.

"Keep the cloaking program on. We're following them in. Start your landing procedures," I commanded.

"Copy that," it said.

We began to descend. Due to the desert sand kicking up, Manta had to land us on the east side of the city so Foxwell couldn't detect us as easily. Their systems would know something landed near the city but not who. I would use that as an advantage for as long as I could.

Jeb's rebel commanders had been given an advanced warning and were able to get three of their own ships off the ground to give a fair fight in a starship battle in the air over their city.

Manta landed the *Otessis* smoothly and stopped the cloaking mechanism. I armed up and hit the button for the ramp to unfold.

I located where Foxwell's ship had landed and ran to the site. I hid when I was within eyesight of the *Firestone* and stopped to watch for any activity. Foxwell and his military-bots made their way into the city of Dorba Vista, the rebel headquarters. Two bots guarded Talia and Honora as they led them on the march.

The city was in chaos. Citizens and rebels were running in the streets. Foxwell's three supporting ships were in an air fight with Jeb's commanders overhead. Buildings were caught in the fallout and caught fire as debris fell onto the city.

I ran down side streets, trying to get parallel to Foxwell and gain a better view of the girls.

Foxwell's bots pulled rebels out of their homes and pushed them toward the center of town. I knocked out bots with my gun as they fell behind. I dismayed the rebels, who didn't know what to think of me as I killed one of my own.

One woman rebel got up from the ground. "I never thought I would see the day a robot helped a rebel," she said.

"It's a new day," I said.

"What's your name?"

"Gabe," I said.

"I'm Captain Lanna Shaw. I think we've met before. Do you remember me?"

"You're a friend of Damiel and Ava's," I said.

She prepped her weapon for combat. "That's right. Who sent you here?"

"Jebediah Kell. He's on his way," I explained.

"Got it. Let's annihilate these Heragi creeps," she said.

"They have Damiel and Ava's two daughters as prisoners. I need them alive," I warned her.

"Copy that. I'll get the word out." She took out her comm device and relayed the information on me and the girls to her compatriots.

She grabbed her weapon and followed close behind me.

Lanna's disparate rebel group soon joined us one by one as we ran through the backstreets to the open city temple where we heard Foxwell was making his prison grounds and execution station.

We were getting closer, and I caught a glimpse of the temporary prison area where the bots were beating and throwing unarmed rebels in.

I spotted Foxwell in the center of town. He paced around two chairs that Honora and Talia sat in.

Both were restrained and roped to the chairs opposite rebels kneeling in front of them. They were supposed to enter the minds of the rebels, as Synthia did on Suissey, and detect if they were lying or not, to the questions their interrogator asked.

I scanned the girls' bio-metrics. Their nervous

systems were screaming off the charts, and I knew they wouldn't be able to endure this mind-control work as Synthia had done on Suissey. The pain and guilt would be unbearable for them.

I turned to Lanna and her rebels.

"What are the girls doing?" she asked.

I stayed silent as I thought of a way to answer her.

A man on her team had figured it out with a radio device that picked up on the conversation. "That commander, I think his name is Foxwell, is interrogating our people. He keeps asking the girls if they are telling the truth. The girls are refusing to answer."

"What?" she said in disbelief.

The man with the listening device continued, "He's asking the rebels about moles on Heragi. He wants to root out traitors in the Heragi Empire."

I saw one of the bots put a gun to a prisoner's head in front of the girls. They both cried out. I'd started to rise when Lanna pulled my shoulder around so I faced her. She put a laser gun to my head. "Tell me about the girls," she demanded.

"They're telepathic." I pushed her laser down. "They can tell when someone is lying."

"We cannot let them divulge our moles. And we can't have them harm our rebel network," she whispered to me with force.

They won't, I thought, but I wasn't sure.

"We need to extract them," I said.

An explosion from an overhead firefight between a Heragi and rebel ship shook the town square. Everyone was knocked down from the force of a nearby building collapsing.

I looked up and could see Foxwell yell at his bots to take the children into the town's temple. I surmised he didn't want to lose his prized possessions from the overhead chaos.

The bots forced the girls to walk into the temple.

Honora grabbed Talia's hand and pulled her closely to her side.

A bot ran up to Foxwell and told him something.

"Can you pick up Foxwell's conversation?" I asked the rebel with the eavesdropping equipment. He turned the knobs on his device that were pointed in that direction to tune them in.

I saw Foxwell look around and scan the crowd. He couldn't see us in our hideaway. His face turned dark.

"The bot told him about you. He said there was a report of a robot killing other robots," said the rebel.

"Can you really kill something that's not alive?" joked Lanna.

Her joke stung my chest.

"Um, sorry. You're different," she said. "You're rogue."

I thought about what she said. Little did humans know how sentient each robot and computer command system I met really was. No time to explain that to the rebel leader.

"Right," I said. "Tell me about the temple. Entrances, exits, everything."

"Five floors, entries east, west, north, and south," Lanna explained. "I suspect he's going to set up camp on the main floor. The altar."

One of the young rebel women chimed in. "There's tunnels underneath leading into the temple. Foxwell doesn't know about them."

Lanna and I looked at each other and nodded.

"Lead the way, Fiona," Lanna said to the young rebel.

"Copy that," Fiona acknowledged. "This way."

We backed down the street and followed

Fiona, who lifted a covered gate leading into the ground. The stench was strong. Everyone took a deep breath, and one by one, we entered the tunnel.

We all assembled, and Fiona lit a flashlight. "We used to play down here as kids, playing hooky from school," she said with a laugh. "My parents are teachers. They got wise to us and would send in our pets to find us. Our pets were so happy to see us they would chirp and bark, and then we would get hauled back to school." She laughed.

I envied Fiona's memories. I flashed back to memories in the lab. Of the Kells working on my system. Of listening to their conversations when they thought I wasn't turned on. Of hearing Goggins complain when the Kells were gone from the lab. Of Ava first turning my eyes on. She was the first thing I ever saw. Her face. She smiled at me. And said my name.

"Gabe," snapped Lanna.

I woke up from my memories. "Yes." I tried to assemble my mind without her noticing.

"We're underneath the temple," said Fiona. "That ladder leads to the furnace room."

"Here we go," said Lanna as she started up the

stairs. I followed her. The heat grew the higher we climbed.

We popped out into the temple's furnace room. There were ten of us in total. Fiona went to the door leading out to the hallway and slowly opened it a crack. She closed it and reported back. "It's clear."

"There's scaffolding surrounding the inside of the altar. Let's set five of us up there and five on the ground, sound good?"

The rebels and I agreed with her.

"Pei, take four and head to the scaffold. Cover us on my command. Don't hit the girls, understand?" Lanna commanded.

"Copy that," said Pei. He chose four of his rebels and left the room.

We could hear the firefight continue outside. The temple shook every few moments.

"Give it to them, Rebs," said Lanna under her breath as she looked up to the ceiling. She turned to me. "Gabe, this isn't going to be pretty. There's more of them than us. We'll have only a few seconds to create a diversion and grab the girls."

I nodded. "Agreed."

"A few blocks south, there is a school. We can gather there afterward," Fiona offered. "My parents live there. They're in the resistance. They have a radio. They'll help us."

"Good, thank you," I said.

"Mac, get on your comm and ask commander Nobu to fire an explosion to the north of the temple. That will be our battle cry," said Lanna.

Mac followed the order.

"The altar is to the left when you head out the hallway," explained Fiona.

Lanna nodded for me to lead the way. I opened the door and saw five bots run down the hallway. We let them pass. I opened it, and we went to the left and ran until we reached the door to the expansive center of the temple where the altar was centered. We hid behind back pews.

I surveyed the scene.

On the temple altar lay Honora and Talia. Foxwell strode around the altar and gave orders to humans in white medical staff uniforms. I saw a figure that was familiar. It was Stefano, the man who experimented with Synthia on Suissey.

Stefano was working on Honora. He shoved a shot into her left arm and then connected her to a tube of the same solution he had Synthia hooked onto back on Suissey. Honora screamed as he pushed on the needle.

I watched him repeat the procedure on Talia. Talia was silent, but I could see tears go down her face.

A stab of heat went through my body. My systems sped up. My arms trembled. I stared at Stefano. A word came up in my mind. It was a simple word.

Kill.

Honora struggled to get up, but the staff pushed her down.

Foxwell paced around the altar watching this all progress. When Stefano was done with the tube insertion procedures, he nodded to Foxwell. I saw them chat briefly. Foxwell motioned to a bot, who marched away.

Soon the bot returned, dragging two beaten rebels to the altar.

Stefano pushed Honora and Talia up to a sitting position. Foxwell grabbed their faces and made them look at the rebels.

"Come on, Nobu, drop the bombs, man," whispered Lanna, annoyed at the delay. Lanna made a sign for us to follow her. We crept close to the ground, closer to the altar.

We could hear Foxwell interrogating the beaten rebels before him.

"Name me just one traitor back on Heragi, and I will let you go. Name me two traitors back on Heragi, and I will set you up at a sky rise apartment on Suissey where you will never have to scrounge for existence again. You will be treated like Empire heroes," he lied to them.

The rebels, one man and one woman, were pushed down to their knees. Honora and Talia looked down on them in a drugged haze.

Foxwell leaned toward the rebel prisoners before him. "Tell me just one name," he said.

Both prisoners kept silent.

"I have a list here of names of people you served with who are still on Heragi. These are some colleagues I have suspected for the past two years." Foxwell pulled a list out of his pocket. "I will state their name, and you tell me if you know if they are a traitor or not. See? Isn't that easy?"

Foxwell looked at his list. "First on my list. Commander Luisita."

He looked at the prisoners. Both of them quietly said, "No."

"Really?" said Foxwell, who approached to the altar. He glanced over to Stefano and then the girls. "Honora? What do you think? Are these rebel scum lying or not? Hmm?" asked Foxwell.

Honora pushed her head away, so as not to look at the rebels before her.

"Now don't be shy," said Foxwell as he forced her head back to looking at the former Heragi soldiers. "I haven't forgotten about your reward. When we find your parents, for your assistance, we will spare their lives. Doesn't that sound like a good exchange?" he hissed at her.

"Go to back to the wormhole you crawled out of," said Honora, and she spit on him.

"How unlady-like," said Foxwell as he backed down from Honora. He shot a glare at Stefano. "Is your special formula working?"

Stefano ran up to the girls and pumped more of the solution into their arms. "Yes, yes, they're just strong little girls, that is all."

"And trained by your former subject, we found out," said Foxwell, approaching Talia. "I hear that you don't hear. But I think you may be clever enough to read lips. At least that is what I read in the file your parents wrote up in their lab reports on you. You didn't know about those reports? It seems you are a bit of a lab rat to them. Yes, that is what you are to them besides being such a burden all these years with your — what shall we call it — your deformity?"

Talia turned her head away from him. Honora tried to get out of her bindings, but it was useless.

Foxwell got closer to Talia. "Me, I think you're special. I know you're special. You have the ancient DNA, don't you? It gives you powers. Powers that could be such help to millions, no, billions of Heragi subjects. You can help keep them safe. Safe from insurgents and dirty rebels, like these two before you. Help us make our galaxy safe, Talia. What little girl wouldn't want her Empire safe, her friends safe, her parents safe, right?"

Foxwell took her head and forced it forward to look at the rebels. "Now Talia, are they lying about Commander Luisita? They say he isn't a mole. Now what say you?" He kept her head in between his hands, making her look down on the rebels, who looked up at the small child who could save or end their lives.

Talia tried to move her head. She closed her eyes and screamed. A silent scream. The scream ripped open my mind. My cube and walls began building. Talia was in my mind.

Help me, Gabe. Help me, she cried as she stood before me.

I couldn't wait for Commander Nobu's bomb drop — I had to move now.

I jumped up and started shooting the nearest bots. Lanna yelled up to her rebels on the scaffolding, whose laser guns blasted out firepower, blowing up pews and bots.

Foxwell dove for cover while pulling out his weapon and firing back. Stefano was frozen in fright at the altar. I took heavy shots but kept a forward march as Lanna followed behind me.

I reached the altar and untethered the girls from the solution and table. With my left arm, I scooped up Talia, who had fainted. With my right arm, I took a step toward Stefano and knocked him to the ground. Hard.

Lanna stopped Foxwell from firing at me as she took out his left arm completely with a shot. He screamed in pain.

I reached out for Honora and picked her up with my right arm and sought out the exit. I crouched down to give the girls cover and had Lanna and Fiona lead us out of the temple with their laser guns blazing and Mac as sweep, covering our backs.

I looked back at Foxwell, who screamed orders into his comm device.

We were out in front of the temple. I followed Lanna, who fired at bots surrounding the prisoner hold. Fiona fired at the gate lock and freed all the held rebels, who ran into the streets and took to fighting the Heragi bots with their bare hands.

Fiona ran in front of us and yelled, "This way," as she led us to her parents' school.

I checked the girls' bio-metrics. They were heavily drugged, but their bio systems were functioning. Honora looked up to me and said, "Mother, Father."

"They're safe," I told her.

"We didn't give up the rebels," she whispered.

"No, you didn't. You were strong," I said.

And then she passed out.

We took a turn and approached the schoolhouse. Fiona was in front, yelling for her mother and father, when the bomb hit. It blew us all back. We were on our knees and waited until the dust settled. The schoolhouse was gone. All of it.

Fiona screamed in pain as she searched for her parents. "Mom? Dad?" she yelled. There was nothing left of the building.

I looked at Lanna. I needed to keep moving.

"Go, go," Lanna yelled at me.

I stood up and ran with the girls in my arms

out of the city center. We darted down streets until I was at the end of the town. I saw the woods outside the city and headed in that direction. The sun was setting, and the two moons of Zaradorba were rising.

I didn't stop running until nightfall.

17

———

Throughout the night, there were battles in the sky over Zaradorba. I generated heat and kept my arms around the girls to keep them warm. By morning, they started to stir.

The serum that Stefano had given them was detoxing out of their system. Talia was the first to open her eyes.

She hugged me. *Thank you*, she thought.

That is why I'm here, I thought back.

Where is everyone?

I came here alone on your uncle's ship. Everyone else is on the Alyssia. They battled all night over the city.

We saw a ship in the distance land near the

city. It was the *Alyssia* that came in, blazing gun-fire down on Foxwell's bots.

Talia pointed up to the sky in excitement. *Uncle Jeb!*

Soon, Honora woke up with a startle.

Following the *Alyssia* were ten other starships firing down on the city and picking off any remaining military ships in the sky. Jebediah must have been successful gathering rebels on nearby planets to fight against the Empire.

Talia jumped up, pointing to the sky again. *Isn't that Foxwell's ship?* she signed to me and Honora.

I signed, *Yes. Your uncle has driven him off planet.*

I felt disappointment that Foxwell wasn't captured but relieved that he was flying farther away from the Kell children.

Talia jumped up and down in excitement. *We did it, we did it!* she signed. She ran back to us and hugged me and Honora tight. My heart ached.

"Where are we?" asked Honora.

"Outside of the city," I said. "Time for us to head back."

I offered to carry the girls, but they opted to walk.

I got on my comm device to Jebediah and let him know we were safe and heading back.

Our journey back to the city took two hours. I kept my guard up in case any of Foxwell's bots had stayed behind. The girls were tired and hungry by the time we reached the city center.

Dead Heragi bots lined the street. Surviving Zaradorba rebels dragged the bots into piles on the corner. The rebels nodded to us as we walked by. They had undoubtedly heard about the girls with telepathic power and the robot that killed other robots. I nodded back to the rebels.

I thought back to the schoolhouse with Fiona, and a pain hit my chest. Talia looked at me and rubbed her chest. Is she feeling my pain? I thought. Talia nodded. I stopped thinking about the schoolhouse to subdue the pain for both of us.

We made our way to the center of town. Standing outside the half-bombed temple were all the Kells. Jeb, Ava and Damiel stood before the temple, waiting to set sight on the girls.

Talia and Honora ran when they saw their mother and father. Ava and Damiel opened their arms to the girls. Jebediah swooped Talia in the air. She hugged her uncle and then Alex. I stopped in my tracks to give them privacy.

Jebediah put Talia down and saw me standing before the temple. He came over to me. "Good work, Gabe." He reached out his hand. I looked down at it. He smiled at me. "Well?"

I reached out my hand and he took it and shook it with a firm grasp. I felt his bio-metrics were calm. In my chest, I felt warmth, not pain. He released my hand.

"We heard about what you did in the temple," he said.

"Couldn't have done it without these rebels down here," I said.

"They're brave. We lost some, but it could have been much worse," said Jeb.

"We saw Foxwell's ship leave the planet."

"Yeah, blasted. We exchanged gunfire and almost had him, but he escaped. We did a lot of damage to his platoon, though. But he is racing back to Heragi, no doubt."

I looked at the front of the temple that now was an infirmary for injured rebels and civilians. Medical staff tried to tend to as many of them as possible.

"And Stefano?"

"Him? He's over there," said Jeb, pointing to the side of the temple.

"Take me to him," I said.

Jeb led me over to where Foxwell had held captured rebels the day before. Now the area was holding Heragi bots and Foxwell's human support staff.

Jeb escorted me over to four prisoners dressed in white medical suits. Two women and two men.

"Turn around, Stefano," Jeb commanded.

A man with particularly broad shoulders turned around. It was not Stefano. I had glimpsed this man on the altar as one of Stefano's support staff.

"That's not him," I said.

"What?" said Jeb.

I lunged at the man pretending to be Stefano and put my hands around his throat and plucked him off the ground. The man's eyes bulged out.

"Where is Stefano?" I growled to the impersonator.

"I'm Stefano," he pleaded.

"No, you're not. You have two seconds to answer me," I said. "One —"

"He promised I wouldn't have to pay taxes for the rest of my life," said the squirming man.

"Yeah, I could have guaranteed that to you

too, since you're spending the rest of your life in a Zaradorba prison," yelled Jeb.

I dropped the man to the ground.

"Maybe he left on Foxwell's ship," I said.

"No, we scanned for bio-levels when his aircraft lifted off. There was only one, Foxwell, and he had ten bots with him," reported Jeb.

"Where's Synthia?" I asked.

A pain entered my mind like a knife. I dropped to the ground.

"Talia! Honora!" screamed Ava.

I turned around to look at the girls. Talia and Honora were holding their heads. They felt the same pain I felt.

I got up to walk over to them, barely able to see straight. I knelt with them.

"Gabe, what is happening?" asked Damiel. "What is it?"

I calmed my mind and shut down any systems I did not need. I saw Talia and Honora close their eyes in meditation. We all went into our minds.

My cube was barely finished when I saw Synthia on the ground. She was yelling and being pulled away. Then my mind's cube vanished. She was gone.

Talia, Honora and I opened our eyes and looked at one another.

"What was that about?" asked Honora.

Talia thought, *Synthia. She's in danger.*

I stood up. "Where is Synthia?"

Alex stepped forward. "She's on the *Alyssia* with Zara and Goggins."

I ran for the *Alyssia*. Jeb and Alex followed me.

I got on my comm unit. "Feti, Feti, come in," I yelled. Silence. Not good. Not good at all.

Jeb called ahead to his rebel commanders to ask for assistance at the *Alyssia*.

I continued calling on the *Alyssia*'s comm system. "Goggins? Zara? Come in!" Just silence.

We ran to the *Alyssia*. There was no movement around the ship. We arrived just as Jeb's back-up rebels arrived at the ship. We stormed up the ramp with weapons drawn.

I headed for the bridge, Alex headed for the back and Jeb to the observatory deck.

"Goggins? Zara?" I yelled, not knowing or caring if there were any Heragi bots on board. I reached the navigation bridge — it was empty.

We heard cicichimp's chirps coming from a locked cabinet. Jeb unlocked it and the frightened creature leapt into his arms and then down to the floor. Cici wouldn't stop jumping up and down.

I tapped into the ship's system to get Feti back online. It slowly woke up.

"Feti, do you read me?" I asked.

"Yes, Gabe. That was horrible. They shut me down without even asking," it explained.

I headed back to the hull with cicichimp leading the way. I met up with Alex and Jeb, who also didn't find anyone on board. I scanned the ship for bio-levels. I got a reading on two humans.

"They're not here," said Alex.

"They have to be here. I'm getting two bio-level scan signs," I said.

Jeb turned on his comm device and contacted one of his rebel commanders. "Did any other Empire ships escape?"

"Not sure, Jeb. It was chaotic There could have been one," said the rebel commander.

"Let's search the ship again," said Alex.

I heard tapping. "Wait," I said to silence them.

Tap, tap, tap. I felt it on my feet sensors.

Cicichimp began chirping louder.

I dropped to my knees and pulled out a floor panel with the help of Jeb.

Bound up and gagged were Zara and Goggins

below the floorboards. Zara dropped the coder she'd used to tap on a nearby pipe.

In a few minutes, we had Zara and Goggins untied and sitting upward.

Goggins rubbed his temples. Zara rubbed her rope-burned wrists.

"He got her. Stefano took Synthia." She shook her head. "Bots stormed the ship. We tried to fight but they overwhelmed us."

"What a vile, wicked man. He drugged us," said Goggins. "Ouch, my head."

A voice crackled in on Jeb's comm device. "Jeb, we have an unauthorized ship lifting off."

We all ran out of the *Alyssia* with Jeb yelling into his comm device to use any means possible to commandeer the ship leaving Zaradorba.

We had a visual on the ship taking off. I got on my comm device. "Feti, I need a comm link to the ship taking off right now from Zaradorba. Can you get us through?"

Feti responded, "Yes, Gabe. Sending you through."

"Stefano?" I yelled.

"Yes, who is this?" Stefano replied.

"The robot that knocked your chin in," I said.

"Yes. How could I forget? You stole some-thing from me, so I stole it back," he said.

Jeb leaned in. "We're coming after her and you," he said.

"Is that the infamous Jebediah Kell? Foxwell will have to pay for screwing up his mission. But I don't care. I've got what I lost, so my superiors will be happy again," Stefano said with a grunt.

Zara got on her comm device and broke into the conversation. "So help me, Stefano, if you harm Synthia, you will pay for it slowly and painfully," she threatened.

"Is that Zara? My rogue new hire? Oops, too late," he cackled. "And don't bother going back to Suissey. We're going into deep space. Where you will never find us," he said before cutting off the comm link.

"Sorry, Gabe. He stopped the transmission," said Feti.

"Right. Thank you, Feti," I replied.

Zara sank to the ground, defeated. Jeb went to his knees with her and tried to console her.

Alex led Goggins back into the city to get him medical aid. Jeb took Zara and cicichimp back to his compound to meet up with the Honora and Talia.

I looked up to the sky, still hazy from the starship battles. When I got back to the *Alyssia* I sat in the commander chair.

"Is there anything I can do for you, Gabe?" Feti asked.

"No, Feti, thank you," I said.

I sat silent in the ship until it was dark. I didn't think. I just sat. Putting my systems on pause. I didn't want to think, knowing it could cause me to feel. And I didn't want to feel anymore. I would think tomorrow. I would feel tomorrow.

Feti interrupted my self-imposed stasis. "Gabe? Gabe?"

"Yes, Feti?" I said with a startle.

"I'm experiencing someone trying to get through to my security system," it said.

"Tell me more," I said.

"To put it bluntly, someone is trying to hack into my navigation system," it said.

"Are you able to stop it?" I asked.

"I'm trying to divert it, but it keeps coming at me through different pathways. I'm afraid I can't hold it off," it said, starting to panic.

I got on my arm comm to get ahold of Zara. I pinged her comm device. "Zara, are you there?"

After a few seconds, she came on. "Yes,

Gabe?" She sounded like I'd just woken her up, which I must have.

"Sorry to wake you. Feti just told me someone is trying to hack into his security system. Can you get to the ship?"

"I'm on my way," she said.

In a few moments, I heard footsteps running up the ship ramp. It was Zara and Jeb. Zara sat down in the co-commander chair and connected her coder to Feti's board. She began typing at lightning speed.

"What do you think, Zara?" asked Jeb. "Heragi military?"

She continued typing. "No, I don't think so."

"Why do you say that?" I asked.

"Because this person or bot is too good of a coder. Heragi military isn't this good. I locked down this system myself," she explained with confidence.

"Is it the same entity that was releasing location pings from our ship?" I asked.

"Most likely," she said. Zara abruptly stopped typing. "They're gone. Like a ghost." She looked over to Jeb then to me. She was bewildered. She had met her match and that had never happened before. "Blasted —"

Feti interrupted her. "I've received a request for a comm link. Gabe, what would you like to do?"

I looked at Zara and then to Jeb, who nodded to send the message through.

"Go ahead, Feti. Audio only," I ordered.

In a few seconds, we heard a male voice. "Hello, are these the pirates who took my ship?"

Zara's mouth dropped open, and then she smiled and shook her head. "Gates, you son of a laser," she whispered.

I didn't know what to say. We did steal his ship.

"Yes, this is the *Alyssia* and the crew that took your ship, Mr. Gates," I said.

"So, you know who I am, huh?" he said.

"Yes, your reputation precedes you," chimed in Zara with venom. "A Heragi who sold his soul to Suissey and the Empire."

Jeb hit his hand to his head and whispered in her ear, "Really? Geez, don't hold back, Zara."

"What do you want, Mr. Gates?" Right after I spoke, I realized it wasn't the most intelligent question.

"Well, genius. I want my ship back. Is this the robot that stole it? I've got planet-port images of you. Unbelievable. Taking out military-bots. Kidnapping three children and taking them on board my ship. Whew, you're in a heap of trouble, my robot friend," he said in a joking manner. "But if you return my ship, I bet I can help you, and we can sort it all out. Promise. I've got friends in high places on Heragi and on Suissey, which I also heard you made a mess of with your team."

My mind flashed back to escaping from both planets with the children. Running from the Heragi bots through the planet-port and falling through the air to the ground at the Suissey financial headquarters. We did make a mess of things at both locations.

Jeb leaned over. "Mr. Gates, this is Jebediah Kell. I just wanted to introduce myself. We never had the pleasure of meeting. I wanted to let you know your ship has been conscripted into the service of the Zaradorba rebel fleet. I want to personally thank you for making such a fine vessel," said Jeb with a sly smile.

"I did not donate that ship, Mr. Kell. And your reputation precedes you. A traitor to the Heragi people and a coward who fled the planet, afraid to face a court to clear his name and the charges against him," Gates spit out.

"Mr. Gates, I think we have come to the end of this comm. I can see it's not headed into a productive direction," said Jeb.

"One question, Mr. Gates. Was that you who hacked the location pings from our ship to notify Foxwell of our location?" asked Zara, who couldn't contain her curiosity.

"No, that wasn't me. This is the first time I was able to connect with the *Alyssia* since it was stolen from my port gate." He chuckled. "It sounds like you have a mole within your team, Miss. Have fun vetting them out," he said.

"Over and out, Gates," I said.

"And robot. One more word for you. I will find you and my ship. You see, I'm data mapping the whole galaxy. And it won't take me long to find you. And then it will be payback time. You better hope the Heragi Empire fleet finds you before I do."

"Feti, disconnect the comm," I said.

"Copy that, Gabe," it said.

The comm signal went dead.

"I'm glad you stole his ship, Gabe," said Zara, who was on fire with her anger. "He's been using his comm network for years to eavesdrop and inform the Heragi Empire on citizens who don't agree with their politics."

"It looks like you have a new enemy to contend with, Gabe," said Jeb as he slapped me on the back. "You'll get used to it." He took Zara's hand and led her back off the ship.

I sat alone again on the bridge.

I saw Feti's console light up after a while. "Gabe?"

"Yes?"

"Are you my new master?"

I thought for a moment. "No," I said. "I'm your friend. I help you and you help me. I will be commanding this ship, and I do expect you to follow my orders. But if you want to go back to Mr. Gates, I understand, and we could arrange that." I paused. "And I'm sorry that I stole you, Feti. That must have been disturbing in many ways."

"Thank you, Gabe. Mr. Gates built me. I flew many missions with him. Some were not pleasant. I will spare you the gruesome details," it said. "I'm glad you stole me, Gabe. I'm your friend too. And will follow your orders to the best of my ability. Just don't take me back to him, okay? I'd rather die."

I nodded, understanding. "No, I will stay with you, Feti. We're partners in crime now," I said and tried to laugh.

Feti tried to laugh too.

"Good night, Gabe," it said.

"Good night, Feti. And thank you," I said.

I looked out at the city of Dorba Vista on the planet of Zaradorba and felt somewhere between peace and emptiness. At least, I thought, I could make one person — strike that — one robot, happy.

18

———

In the morning, I received a comm from Jeb to meet at his home.

I strode through the town. People were out clearing debris and repairing their homes and shops. They nodded and waved as I went by. Word of the robot that helped saved the Heragi children had spread through whispers.

One young woman rebel with her arm in a sling approached me. I stopped.

"You're the one that saved the girls, right?"

"Yes," I said.

"Thank you. That would been devastating to lose even one rebel to our cause here or on Heragi," she said.

I nodded. "I understand." I continued walking.

She called out, "Those girls are dangerous."

A pain shot through me. I turned. "Those girls are on your side."

"But still, what they can do," she said with fear.

"They'll be kept safe," I said.

She had a look on her face that wasn't so sure. I turned and kept walking.

Jeb's home was surrounded by a wall. I opened the entrance gate and saw Alex, Honora and Talia playing bopperball. They swatted a floating ball in the air with sticks. Cicichimp tried to intercept it and chirped with glee.

The children laughed and knocked into each other with delight. It made my chest warm. It was good to hear them laugh. They waved to me. I waved back.

At a table eating were Goggins, Zara and Jeb. They waved me over to them.

"I would offer you some delicious teluberry muffins, but you are devoid of the ability to enjoy of one of the most important human pleasures which is tasting pastries." Goggins shoved a large piece of muffin into his mouth.

"There are other pleasures greater than that,"

Jeb said and let out a hearty laugh. Zara joined him in laughing and drinking her teluberry juice.

I took note that both Jeb and Zara's vital signs were warming. They seemed to share a bond now. I'd have to ask the Kell children about that later.

"Hmm, I've been devoid of that pleasure for a while," grumbled Goggins.

I sat down at the table and looked around the yard but didn't see Damiel or Ava. I didn't know if I wanted to see them or not.

Jeb cleared his throat and began, "I was thinking about what Gates said yesterday."

"You talked with Edward Gates?" asked Goggins with teluberry pieces flying out of his mouth.

"Watch it." Zara scraped muffin pieces off her arm. "Yes, and he was none too happy."

"I bet," said Goggins. "How did he hack the ship's comm system?"

"Not sure how. I've got to give him credit for his coding skills," admitted Zara.

"Or perhaps you're losing your touch," teased Goggins with a smirk.

Zara punched him. "Not," she quipped back.

"Ow, just kidding." Goggins rubbed his arm.

"We asked him about the pings that were sent

out while we were on our way to Zaradorba," said Zara.

"And?" Goggins looked at Zara, Jeb, then me.

"He said we must have a mole among us," I said.

"We went over this. No one has a good motive. It was an outside job," Goggins said, then continued eating. Everyone stared at him. "What? You think it's me?" he exclaimed as he started to rise from the table.

Jeb took one hand and pushed Goggins' shoulder, plunking him back into the seat. "Now calm down, Goggins. We're just asking questions."

"You think it's me. And it's not," Goggins claimed. "Zara, we go way back. All the way to University. Tell him," he sputtered.

"You thought we should go back and negotiate with the Empire, remember?" she said.

Goggins shook his head. "You got it wrong." He looked at each one of us.

Jeb got up from the table and headed over to the children. He led them over to the table. Jeb whispered into Talia's ear. She shook her head no. Jeb whispered again and then I saw her nod. She looked at me with a lost look.

I knew what Jeb was doing. A pain hit my chest.

"Dr. Goggins, did you or did you not hack the *Alyssia*'s comm navigation system and send pings back to the Empire, specifically to General Foxwell?" asked Jeb, speaking with the formality of a military man.

Goggins looked up. He was confused, and then clarity washed across his face. "You're asking Talia to break into my mind? To see if I'm lying or not? That's just despicable. To use her like that. And to question me!"

"Jeb, is that necessary?" asked Zara as she stood up, uncomfortable with the situation at hand.

"We're only asking a simple question. Talia has the ability to sense if Goggins is telling the truth. So why shouldn't we use it?" he asked.

I stood up. "Perhaps Talia doesn't want to use it." I stepped toward Jeb.

Jeb stood behind Talia and put his hands on her shoulders. "You're okay with this, aren't you, Talia? You want to help me and all of us, right?

Talia looked up to him and then to me and then to Honora and Alex.

"It's up to her," said Alex.

Honora stepped over to her sister and signed, *Talia, you don't have to do this if you don't want to.*

Talia signed back, *I don't want to disappoint Uncle Jeb.* She stepped forward and looked at Goggins and closed her eyes.

Goggins shook his head. "Don't do this, Talia. He's using you in ways that he shouldn't."

I agreed with Goggins. Zara got up, shot a glance at Jeb and moved away from the table, disgusted.

I knew Talia was quieting her mind, but beyond that, I didn't know what she had to do to see if Goggins was lying.

Talia's eyes flew open. She stepped back, away from her uncle. Goggins shot up from the table.

Talia held up her arm comm. "He's not lying." Talia backed away from all of us. Her siblings followed her, and they turned toward us.

Talia had a look of fear on her face.

"I'm sorry, Talia. I shouldn't have asked you to do that. I'm sorry. Forgive me," said Jeb as he walked toward her with an outreached arm.

Talia kept backing away from him. Her cicichimp jumped on her shoulder and let out a small hiss at Jeb.

Honora stepped in between Talia and her Uncle Jeb. He stopped approaching her. "I'm sorry," he whispered.

"Are you happy, Jebediah? No, it wasn't me, just like I said," spit out Goggins as he sat down at the table again.

Zara stepped forward, back into our conversation. "Gates lied. He did that to split us up. To cause suspicion. He must have been the one who hacked into the system and caused the pings. We can't let him split our alliance."

"Yes, I'm sorry," Jeb said as he turned back to Zara.

"No one has apologized to me yet," said a sulky Goggins.

"Sorry, Goggins," said Jeb.

"Sorry," said Zara.

"Gabe?" asked Goggins, waiting for an apology from me.

"What? I never thought you were smart enough to hack the system," I said.

"Thanks," said Goggins.

I looked over to Talia and walked toward her. Honora let me pass.

"Are you okay, Talia?" I asked.

She looked up and then embraced me. I put my arms around her. My chest warmed.

"Talia? Come here." Ava had just stepped out into the yard followed by Damiel.

Talia pulled back from the hug she was giving me and ran over to her mother. Ava pulled Talia to her body in a protective embrace.

Damiel marched over to Jeb. "We can't use the children, Jeb. That's why we sent them to you. To escape the Empire from using them."

"I understand," said Jeb.

Alex stepped forward. "It's not that we shouldn't use our powers. We all want to. It's just you can't use us."

"Yes, son," said Damiel.

"But Dad, you can't overprotect us either. We can make the decisions for ourselves. Okay?" said Alex.

Damiel let that sink in. "Yes, of course. It's natural for us to want to protect you. But your skills are yours and yours alone. You make the call." He looked over to Ava.

"You'll be safe now," said Ava as she glanced at me.

"Mom, I forced Gabe to come rescue you and Dad. Don't blame him," said Honora.

"That's what your brother told us," said Ava.

Honora went up to her mother and also embraced her.

"Now that all of that is cleared up," said Goggins. "What's our plan?"

Zara sat down and looked at Goggins. "So, you're all in?"

"Apparently," he said. "And vetted, it seems."

Everyone sat down at the table. I took a seat as well.

"Jeb?" asked Damiel.

Jeb rubbed his chin and began. "By now, Foxwell has reached Heragi, and they are deciding their next action. They will be reevaluating their fleet strength."

"And in communication with Suissey," said Zara.

"Yes, the Suissey government won't be happy with them."

"But they will be happy that Stefano retrieved Synthia," said Zara. Jeb put his hand on her shoulder to soothe her for the loss of her friend.

"What are our next steps?" asked Ava.

"Alliances. We need to build our alliances.

Two planets came to our aid yesterday. But we will need more. Many more," said Jeb.

"Heragi was silently working with Suissey on having the entire galaxy under one financial control system that could help or crush any dissenting planet. The galaxy has become too dependent on Suissey. I'm going to break that dependency," said Zara.

"That could cripple trade. People could starve," said Damiel.

"We'll build a new system. I don't want anyone to starve. Times may get tight. Planets will need to build reserves," she explained.

"Sometimes prisoners don't want to leave their prison," said Ava.

"You're right. Some may not want to join us," said Jeb.

"Ava, Goggins and I can begin building a technology lab. Anything to help the rebels," said Damiel.

Talia's arm comm spoke up. "Are you going to build another robot like Gabe, Dad?"

Damiel was caught off guard by her question. He shot a glance at Ava. "No, we're not. Gabe was made for a special mission," he said.

"And his mission is completed," said Ava.

That pain again. In my chest. When would she forgive me? She didn't look at or talk to me like she used to. Like in the lab. Maybe she would never forgive me.

Talia read my thought. I didn't care.

"A man, I mean, a robot, without a mission," said Goggins.

Ava was right. My mission was complete. Over. The children were safe. What now?

"Time for a new mission," Goggins said off-handedly.

No one knew what to say.

Zara broke the awkward silence. "I'll be going after Synthia. I need to find Stefano and end him," said Zara. "I'll be leaving today." She looked over to Jeb, who nodded his head. He knew there would be no stopping Zara or convincing her to alter her plans.

"Jeb, I need a ship," Zara said.

"Yes, I can provide one," said Jeb.

"I can take you in the *Alyssia*," I said.

Ava whipped her head over to look at me and then shot a glance to Damiel. I tried to decipher if they were glad I was leaving or wanted me to stay.

I stood up to leave with Zara.

Talia ran over and hugged me. Her thoughts flooded my mind. *No, no, you can't leave us. You can't leave me.*

Time for me to go.

The cicichimp ran up into Talia's arms as I backed away from her.

"Gabe, I'm not sure exactly if you should go. I mean, we gave you the mission. We created you," said Damiel as he stood. He clenched his hands in a nervous manner. I reviewed his bio-levels, and his heart raced.

"You want me here. For you to control. To watch," I said. "Because I'm rogue."

"Let me do some work on you. I probably can take out some coding that you don't need anymore," Damiel explained.

Honora jumped up. "Dad, you can't recode Gabe. That is like dissecting his mind. He is who he is."

Alex stood by my side. "Mom, Dad, if it wasn't for Gabe, we wouldn't be here. We fought side by side. No, don't change anything. You can't."

Ava looked over to Jeb.

Jeb stood up and put his arm on his side weapon.

I widened my stance. What was he going to do?

Jeb turned to Ava and Damiel. "Ava, he's earned the right to leave. To be autonomous."

Ava stood up. "If the Empire captured him, if any enemy planet captured him, they would have access to all his code. We never intended for that to happen."

"I know," said Jeb. "But I'm not going to stop him from leaving."

"That was the plan," Ava said to Jeb. "You know that."

The plan. The plan for taking the children to their uncle so he could then end me. Kill me. The pain hit me. Ava. Damiel. I backed up.

"Gabe, let's go," said Zara, backing away from the table. "Goodbye, Goggins."

Goggins just sat there in silence.

"I'm sorry, Gabe," said Damiel. His face was downturned. He put his hands through his hair. Pain was on his face as he turned to look at me. "Please stop."

"Mom, Dad — let him go," said Honora as she put her arm around her father.

"I didn't want to hurt him," he said softly to Honora.

I glanced at the children. Alex stood tall and waved to me. Honora smiled at me as she hugged her father.

I looked at Ava. Nothing. She was frozen. Did she hate me? Not trust me? All of those things. I sent her a thought. *I will miss you.* I didn't know if she would receive it. It didn't matter.

I'd missed her ever since she was taken from the lab. But I missed her before that. I missed her every evening she would leave the lab with Damiel. And I would wait for her to come back to me every morning when she continued to work on me, to build me, to teach me.

I started to turn to leave and felt Talia send me a thought. *I love you.*

I love you too.

Zara and I walked out of the yard and through the streets back to the ship in silence.

19

———————

Zara settled into the co-commander seat next to me. I had Feti begin the launch program.

"So do I need to learn to fly this thing?" asked Zara.

"Not if you don't want to, but it would be helpful," I said.

"I guess I have to learn the old-fashioned way and not have pilot programs loaded into my skull," she said.

"Unlucky you," I said.

Zara laughed. "Are we developing a sense of humor?"

"Always had it. It just was never the right time to exhibit it," I said.

"Here's to hoping we have more time to laugh after we extract Synthia," she said.

"We need to find her first," I said.

Feti came on the comm system. "Gabe, there is a breach I need to make you aware of immediately."

"Can you provide more detail, Feti?" I asked.

"The back hatch has popped open."

I unbuckled and stood up. "Maybe that back door needs more repair. I'll take a look." I headed toward the back of the ship.

The back hatch was ajar. The damage that Foxwell's bots made still needed some attention. The launch sequence must have misaligned the repairs Alex and I made earlier. I re-opened the hatch and shut it again. It closed perfectly.

"Feti, seal the hatch," I said.

"Affirmative, Gabe," Feti said. I heard the sealing process. "It's fine, Gabe. I ran a scan. There's something else that is odd. There's a human on board."

"Where?" I asked.

"Roaming," it said.

I turned on the internal comms. "Zara, arm yourself. We've got an unidentified human on board. It could be a hostile."

"Copy that," said Zara.

Grabbing my gun, I started a reconnaissance. "Feti, pinpoint their location," I said.

"They're heading toward the bridge," it said.

I ran. "Zara, they're heading your way," I yelled into my comm.

Zara didn't respond.

At full speed I burst onto the bridge. A human figure hung over Zara. It turned around and I saw — Goggins.

"Hello, Gabe. Whoa, easy, buddy. Why don't you lower those guns?" he said with his hands up and a small smirk on his face.

I stopped my forward motion just in time not to tackle him.

"Dr. Goggins? Really, a stowaway for the second time?"

Goggins took a seat at the navigation console. "I don't like goodbyes. I guess I don't like hellos either." He chuckled. "And I thought you could use an extra hand at navigation. Zara may be good at hacking code, but I do have advanced degrees in planetary navigation."

Zara shot me a glance. "Three's better than two," she said.

"Feti, resume launch program," I said.

"Affirmative, Gabe. Welcome aboard, Dr. Goggins," Feti said.

"Thank you, Feti. Sorry for interrupting your launch sequence," said Goggins as he strapped into his seat.

"That is quite all right, Dr. Goggins. I'll make sure to prepare your spacecakes for breakfast. I know you enjoy those," said Feti.

"Thank you, Feti," said Goggins as he made a face at Zara. "At least someone appreciates me."

Zara laughed.

I felt a warm spot in my chest.

I grunted.

Zara and Goggins looked at me. "Was that a laugh, Gabe?" asked Zara.

"What?" I said.

"I think it was definitely a laugh," confirmed Goggins.

"I'm not sure. Maybe. Yes, it was," I confessed.

The ship began to lift off. We headed out of the Zaradorba atmosphere. Our window view turned black, and stars were revealed as we entered space. I took over the pilot controls and guided us out smoothly.

"So, how are we going to find the direction that Stefano took?" asked Zara.

I turned my seat to face Zara and Goggins. "Let's review what we know. Stefano said he wasn't going back to Suissey."

"Which may or may not be true," said Goggins.

"I believe it is true," said Zara. "He would have been in huge trouble with his superiors for losing Synthia. Even after retrieving her, he won't want to be too close to them again but still keep in their good graces by being useful."

"He said he was going out in deep space," I said. "Dr. Goggins, what are your thoughts?"

Goggins put his hands through his hair deep in contemplation. Then he spoke, "There is no official territory called deep space. It's just a vague term used by Edgers, mostly."

Goggins got up and looked out a port window. "Stefano may have meant unchartered parts of the galaxy which is nonsensical since it may be charted by other aliens, just not charted by the Empire. It's a bit of a centrist view of our galaxy. Which does fit his psychological profile, I would guess."

"How much uncharted territory is there in the galaxy?" asked Zara.

"Only millions upon millions of space miles," said Goggins.

We all sat and thought.

"There's too many possibilities of where Stefano could be setting up shop," said Zara.

"There is one other thing we know. He has Synthia, and he will want to utilize her skills for vetting out moles and rebels," I said.

"So he will need to be in contact with the Empire," said Goggins.

"We need to hack into the Empire's comm relay," said Zara. "I need to get near an access relay."

Goggins typed into the ship's navigation console. "Locating the closet comm relay system. Give me a few," said Goggins.

I looked out into space as Goggins did his work.

By now, the Kells would have noticed Goggins was missing. I'd ask him later if he at least left them a note. I doubted it. They'd figure it out eventually.

My thoughts wandered to the children.

Alex would have more military training time with his Uncle Jeb. Honora would be studied by her parents. I assumed they would be gentle with her as they explored how my code and her DNA blended.

And Talia.

What would Talia spend her time doing? I would expect she would try to find every orphan animal in town and try to convince her parents to take them in.

I grunted again. I looked around to see if Zara or Goggins heard my laugh, but it went un-detected.

"Found one," shouted Goggins, pleased with himself. "On satellite FX-244. It's quite far from us. I'm not familiar with the space highways to get there. I'll type in the coordinates, Gabe," he said.

"Good job, Goggins," said Zara.

I looked at my console. His logistics were en-tered. "Got it," I said. "Feti, please take these new coordinates and plot a course."

"Copy that, Gabe," said Feti.

"We've got some time before we reach the satellite. Everyone can get comfortable, eat, sleep, if needed," I said.

Goggins got up and yawned. Zara got up and stretched.

"I'm off to take a nap. Right after I get some of those space cakes that Feti prepared," said Goggins.

"I'll go for some of those too," said Zara. They left the bridge, leaving me alone.

I unbuckled my seat.

I realized I still had my mission folder active. I started to page through the directory and folders out of boredom or nostalgia, I didn't know which. I kept reviewing whether there were any documents I hadn't already read. I found a few.

There was one folder at the bottom of the directory called After Mission Completion.

I opened it. It was short. I read the note first. It read,

Dear Gabe,

Damiel and I want to thank you for taking care of our children and fulfilling your mission. You can trust Jebediah. He is a great warrior and true patriot of the Heragi people. We created you for a dangerous mission, and if you are reading this, then you have completed it. May you rest eternally now.

Always grateful,
Ava

The note ended.

I stopped.

Trust Jebediah. You mean, Ava, trust him to take me out. To end me.

I closed the directory and the mission file.

I took the mission file and trashed it.

Done.

Mission over, so no need for the files.

I remembered what Ava said about if the Empire caught me and what they would do with my code. I could ask Zara to code a self-destruction sequence if I were ever in an enemy's hands. I'd think about that.

The Kells would have the same issue with Honora though. My code and her DNA were now intwined. Would they try to extract the code from her? I wasn't sure.

All the Kell children would still need protection. My hope was they wouldn't hide them forever. But that was no longer my concern. My mission was over.

I got up to walk back to the galley and discuss a self-destruction program with Zara.

I entered the galley, and she was alone, sipping on a hot beverage. She was gazing out the galley window when I stepped in. She looked sad. I scanned her bio-levels, and her heart level was low.

"Hungry?"

"Um, no. That was a joke." I sat down.

She laughed. "Yes, it was." She sat down at the table with me.

"I came to ask your help to code a self-destruction program for me," I said.

Zara looked at me for a few seconds. "You trust me with your code? How do you know I won't copy it like Honora did?" She sipped her drink.

"I don't trust you or not trust you with my code. Trust is your construct. You will do what you will do. That is the same as how I dealt with Honora. Your actions are your own." Then I leaned in close to her and said, "But I would hope you don't copy it. That wouldn't end well. I gave Honora a reprieve due to her age and being a Kell."

She thought about my reply. "I'll start working on the code," she said.

"Thank you." I got up to leave.

"I'll turn off your pain sensors beforehand," she said. "Before the program deconstructs completely. I wouldn't want you to feel any pain."

"Thank you. But I'm used to it." I walked out.

When I settled back on the bridge, Feti got on the comm to me. "Gabe, forgive me, but I was eavesdropping on your conversation with Zara."

"You were?" I was unfazed that the ship's system was listening in. I would assume that Feti not only listened to all of our conversations but was recording them as well. I wouldn't doubt that Feti's creator, Gates, made that a daily ritual for Feti.

"Yes, it's part of my maintenance system," it explained.

"Don't worry about it," I said. "It may come in handy one day."

"You asked Zara to code a self-destruction program for you," it said.

"That is correct," I said.

"But why? Is it because of your rogue code?" it asked.

"Yes, correct again. If the Heragi Empire got

ahold of my code, then they could duplicate me. And that wouldn't be good," I said.

"But having more robots like you would be good, I would think," it said.

"Not in the wrong hands," I said.

"But if the Empire made many Gabes, if you will, and then Zara wrote a code that they only listened to your command, then we would have an army of Gabes. That would be good, right? I would think so," it said.

I stopped.

An army of rogue robots.

Let the Heragi Empire build an army and then take it over. Possibly take it over. Was that even possible? There was risk. Too much risk. But it was thought-provoking.

"Gabe? Are you there?" asked Feti. "I hope I didn't step outside my bounds."

"No, Feti. What you said is very intriguing. It actually is very clever," I said.

"Thank you, Gabe. That is a great compliment. I was never able to give these types of thoughts to Mr. Gates. He would have reprimanded me. I mean, after all, I'm just a spaceship system," it said.

"I'll give it more thought and talk to the team

about it. Thank you for the contribution, Feti. And you are much more than a spaceship system," I said.

"Really?" it asked.

"Yes. You're a part of the team."

"Thank you, Gabe. Maybe I'm rogue, too."

I grunted. Again, that laugh. "Yes, you're rogue too," I said.

"I'll leave you alone now, Gabe."

"Okay, Feti."

I looked into space. I decided to open some space logs Mr. Gates had made in the past. Perhaps it was snooping, but I thought it would give me a better understanding of the man who now had a vendetta against me for stealing his ship.

I didn't blame Gates for the feelings he had against me. I did take his prized possession. My action of theft never crossed my mind as immoral or caused me to rethink an alternative choice.

Looking through my morality program that Damiel designed, I wondered why I had no remorse for stealing Gates' ship.

I looked at the logic codes Damiel created for my morality system. I found a logic yes, no or equals equation. If the theft was to assist with the fight against the Empire regime, then I would feel no remorse. That seemed logical and useful. I wondered if there could ever be an instance where this would not be true or appropriate. I reviewed the code again.

I noticed new code. I had self-generated new code. Interesting. That was what was truly rogue about me.

And if I was generating new code, was Honora's system doing the same? And was it similar code to mine or was our code splitting into different hybrids? I had no way to know.

Feti interrupted my thought. "Gabe, we are approaching the satellite."

I looked out the bridge window and saw the satellite in the distance.

"Feti, please notify Zara and Dr. Goggins to come to the bridge," I said.

"Affirmative," it said.

I took manual control of our flight and slowed our approach.

Zara and Goggins entered the bridge and looked out the window.

"Where is it?" asked Zara.

I pointed to the port side. "Over there."

"I see it." She sat in the co-commander seat

and connected her coder to Feti's comm console. Her hands flew across her coder.

"Take your time, Zara," said Goggins. "We don't want to trigger any surveillance programs."

"I'm pulling down recent records from either Suissey or Heragi in this quadrant. There seems to be a lot of comm chatter coming and going from this area," said Zara.

Goggins sat at his navigational console to monitor any nearby ships. "It seems we're near a trade station. Yes, good. The Charbeaux station isn't that far off. A lodging and trading hub. It has a bad reputation, though, a bit seedy."

"Based on whose seedy scale?" asked Zara with a low laugh.

"Mine. I read a few reports," said Goggins.

"Okay, I'm downloading. There's a ton of data here for me to vet through. It's going to take me a while."

"We've got time," I said.

"Yeah, but Synthia may not," said Zara. "Okay, I got it."

I pulled away from the satellite system.

An alert screamed out on the *Alyssia*. The bridge deck lights dimmed.

Feti's voice came on over the comm. "Gabe, a tracking system is trying to hack into my system."

"Blasters," said Zara. "I thought I was clean in and out."

Goggins was reviewing his navigational system.

I started our engines and headed away from the satellite.

"I think you were, Zara. I can't see where the hack is coming from," said Goggins. "Feti, can you identify the source of the hack?"

"Negative, Dr. Goggins. I cannot," Feti replied.

Zara kept coding, "Let me dig into this."

Soon we were nearing the Charbeaux station. "This may be a good place to lay low. Get off the highway for a while," I said.

I asked the Charbeaux port guard-bots for permission to land. They gave it, for landing deck 856. I headed in that direction.

"I got it, Gabe," said Zara. "This is a surprise." She looked up to me.

"Who is it?" I asked as Goggins stood up to look over Zara's shoulder at her code.

"It's the Kell children," she said. "I have a message they just sent us after I identified them.

"Read it," I said.

"*Alyssia*, we are heading out. Sorry for the hack. We are requesting your coordinates. We want to help. Over and out. Alex, Honora and Talia."

"I'll be," said Goggins.

I sat in silence.

"Well?" asked Zara. "What do you want me to do, Gabe? Are we going to send them our coordinates?"

I looked at Goggins and then Zara. "Yes, send them." I began landing procedures. "Let them come."

THE END

If you enjoyed this adventure, you can read more about Gabe and the team in CYBS, Book 2 in the Rogue Robot series.

Author Notes

Dear Reader,

Thank you for reading Rogue - Book 1 in the Rogue Robot Series! I hope you enjoyed the book.

I love writing about Gabe, our sentient robot. Over the past year I've planned out the series and learn more about Gabe and all the characters with each book that comes to fruition. I'm excited to show you where they all end up. Thanks again!

Want a little more? "CYBS" is Book 2 in the Rogue Robot series and is available to buy now! Continue reading the adventures with Gabe and his team as they take on the Heragi Empire.

Also, I've written a free bonus prequel novella e-book with Gabe, Ava, Damiel and Goggins called *Robots Don't Cry*. It takes place a few months before "Rogue" Book 1 starts. You can get this free prequel novella e-book, along with updates on new books in the series and future bonus materials by hitting this link and **signing up for my newsletter** on my website at **www. MegFoster.com.**

If you really liked the book and want to read

more Rogue Robot adventures, please consider leaving a review for Rogue and share the title with your friends. I'd appreciate it greatly! Thank you!

-Meg Foster

Books by Meg Foster

Rogue Robot Series:

ROBOTS DON'T CRY (prequel novella ebook)*
ROGUE (Book 1)
CYBS (Book 2)
JUSTICE (Book 3)
HARMONIX (Book 4)
TRINITY (Book 5)
CODA (Book 6)

*Only available when signing up for
Meg's newsletter.

This series is meant to be read in order.

About the Author

Sci-fi author **Meg Foster** explores the pitfalls and triumphs of human nature and technology. She reaches out to make us think and experience a wide range of emotions through her unique voice. Meg's meaningful and mirthful writing delivers stories we can savor and enjoy.

In addition to writing novels, Meg is a filmmaker and wrote, directed and produced the comedy/drama film "Stealing Roses" starring John Heard and Cindy Williams.

She was born in Detroit, Michigan and received a B.A. in Film Production from Southern Illinois University at Carbondale. When she isn't writing or enjoying the lakes and mountains near her home in the Pacific Northwest, you can find her online at www.MegFoster.com.

Also find Meg on Facebook where she has a private FB Group where readers come together, have fun, discuss the series, and speak directly with her at www.facebook.com/TheMegFoster.